OUTSTAR 1
Dark Discovery

By Samuel McPherson & Richard Criscuola

Outstar 1: Dark Discovery
by Samuel McPherson & Richard Criscuola

All rights reserved. No part of this book may be reproduced (except for inclusion in reviews), disseminated or utilized in any form or by any means, electronic or mechanical, including photocopying, recording, or in any information storage and retrieval system, or the Internet/World Wide Web without written permission from the author or publisher.

Copyright © 2007 by Samuel McPherson & Richard Criscuola

Published by:
Outstar 1
147 West 24th Street
New York, NY 10011

For further information, contact the authors at:
Outstar One@aol.com

Production services provided by:
Celebrity Entertainment Corp.
www.CelebrityEntertainment.org

Book design by:
Arbor Books, Inc.
244 Madison Avenue, #254
New York, NY 10016-2819
(877) 822-2500

Outstar 1: Dark Discovery
by Samuel McPherson & Richard Criscuola
1. Title 2. Author

Library of Congress Control Number 2004104479
ISBN 0-9754132-0-1 (Paperback; $18.95)

DEDICATION

I wish to dedicate this book to my family and friends who have supported this project since day one, and particularly to my grandparents, Louise and Tony Criscuola, who have since departed from our ship.
—Richard Criscuola

I wish to dedicate this book to all my friends who stood by me, my Aunt Tumaini, my cousin Desira, who has since passed, and the rest of my family who encouraged me and told me to never give up.
—Sam McPherson

ACKNOWLEDGEMENTS

We would especially like to thank our editor, Leigh Angel, for her extraordinary effort and patience with us; our equally patient publisher, Larry Leichman, for his dedication to this project; and our production manager, Lisa Mueller, for her invaluable professional advice and encouragement.
—Richard Criscuola and Sam McPherson

1

The Uncharted Planet

THE WARM WIND THAT BLEW across the faces of the OutStar One survey crew had an acrid and lifeless smell. The humid atmosphere of the uncharted planet was thick with death. Chief Operations Officer, Wingate T. Mack, an experienced and highly sought geological engineer, led his crew down the ramp of the NX1 shuttlecraft onto the damp, marshy surface. Their heavy boots sunk into the mud, as they took their first steps.

The light from the planet's only sun was growing dim, casting long shadows across the swamp. Once verdant, now decaying organic outcroppings rose up from the ground like hedgerows, forming wide passageways that created a serpentine labyrinth. In the distance, jagged hills carved a forbidding horizon. There was an eerie silence that put the crew on edge. Except for the occasional rustle of clothing, it was as quiet as deep space.

Chief Mack took out his COMlink from his right breast pocket.

"Chief Mack to OutStar One. OutStar One, do you copy?"

A garbled, barely intelligible transmission came across the chief's communicator.

"OutSt…Command…Lieutenant…Sarwar…over."

"Anjum, I can barely hear you," the chief replied.

"Sir…give…location…" Lt. Sarwar tried.

"Lieutenant, turn on your voice-text translator. We have landed safely on the target planet, referred to hereafter as UC-788. We are about to begin our exploration, but the light is not with us. We may need to be here an extra day. Alert Captain Jones and TESSA. I will contact you again when we are ready to depart. Mack out."

Commander Seth Roberts tapped Chief Mack on the shoulder and pointed to a series of small mounds varying in size from two to three feet in diameter at the base and rising up about two and a half feet, each one generating hot, sulfurous vapor.

"Win, I've never seen, or smelled, anything like this."

The crew, each dressed in khaki pants, the leather flight jacket of OutStar One and equipped with a proton pistol, put on their transparent toxin-filtration masks and gathered around the vapor mounds. Mack turned to face his crew.

"Ladies and gentlemen, the sooner we get the soil samples and core readings, the sooner we can get out of here."

Commander Roberts gathered his security team.

"Giler, Morse and Caffey, scan the area for any signs of animate life. Keep your COMlinks set to frequency Q65 and report any findings. I will take the north quadrant; Giler, take the east; Morse, the west and Caffey, the south."

The security team nodded their acceptance of assignments, adjusted their scancorders and split up. Chief Mack took his remote command cell from the standard-issue instrument transport case that hung from a strap across his chest and activated the shuttle locking sequence. The ramp rose until it was parallel to the ground and slid into its hull, as the door of the shuttle came down covering the entryway with an impenetrable titanium-graphite alloy seal.

"Seth, report back to the shuttle with your team at 18:00 hours and alert us of any potential hazards in the meantime," Chief Mack instructed.

The men shook hands and Commander Roberts walked north through the muck until he was out of sight. Chief Mack called to order his team of scientists and researchers. Lieutenants Fergus and Navalus, experts in geology and surface-to-core analysis, were already recording data on the vapor mounds and taking soil samples. Lieutenant Martinez, a forensic pathologist, and Ensign Ward, a botanist, were investigating the decaying hedgerows.

"Let's work quickly. TESSA needs our findings as soon as possible and will give us an early-completion bonus if we finish ahead of schedule." The chief unzipped his flight jacket to mid-chest to relieve himself from the heat. His blue undershirt was damp with perspiration. "Fergus, Navalus, and Martinez, continue collecting your data. Ward, come with me. I want to see where this path leads."

Scancorders aloft, Chief Mack and Ensign Ward slogged along in a northeasterly direction along one of the many paths marked by the rotting vegetation, careful to avoid the vapor mounds in their way.

"Well, Chief, what do you make of this?" Ensign Ward asked, as she took a scancorder reading of a sticky, fungus-covered branch. "Not a sound, no signs of animation, the intense odor. It's as if this planet is decomposing from the inside out."

"I'm puzzled, I must say," replied the chief.

As they followed the right-leading bend in the path, Chief Mack stopped short in his tracks, sticking his right arm out and catching Ward across the middle.

"What is that?"

The pair of explorers stared at a large depression in the ground—a scorched, sunken oval with three deep slashes through the mire at each end.

"My scancorder indicates that the oval is three and a half meters long, two meters wide, and one and a half meter deep," Ward reported. "The gouges look almost like claw marks, but the surface matter is burnt. Perhaps this is some kind of track or footprint."

"Chief Mack, come in Mack," came Commander Roberts' voice over the COMlink.

"Go ahead, Seth," Chief Mack answered.

"Caffey reports several large charred impressions in the soil in the south quadrant. She says they seem to be the tracks of an animate being, but our scans still show no signs of life."

"Seth, we have discovered the same thing in the labyrinth."

"Sir," Ward called out, "There is another over here." She had walked another ten meters from the first imprint.

"Seth, tell Caffey to gather what information she can in her scancorder and report directly to me if she finds a being to match the markings. Put your crew on high alert. Whatever made these tracks will be colossal and, we have to presume, dangerous. Mack out."

"Yes, sir. Roberts out."

Chief Mack squatted down at the lip of the depression to get a closer look. Ward continued down the path. She contacted Mack with her COMlink.

Chief, I've come across eight more indentations. They appear at intervals of about ten to fifteen meters. Other than the scorched surface matter, no biological residue is apparent."

"Ensign, take a sample of the soil inside one of the prints and let's get back to the shuttle. I've seen enough. We won't have any answers until we can analyze our findings at the lab. Mack out."

"Yes, sir. Ward out."

Chief Mack stood and looked at the sky; a yellow haze clouded the pale sun further diminishing the visibility. A shiver of foreboding crept up his spine.

I must get my crew out of here, Wingate thought. *Their lives are worth more to me than any contract.*

Chief Mack made an announcement to his crew via the COMlink.

"Attention OutStar Research Team. Please conclude your sample collection and report immediately to the NX1 for departure. Mack out."

Ensign Ward came trudging up to Chief Mack. She carried a small, rectangular containment bag from a long strap across her chest. Inside were vials containing soil samples and specimen bags with cuttings from the decomposing hedgerows.

"Chief, I've notice something interesting. The tracks appear out of nowhere and then disappear. The trail begins here, where we're standing and stops about a hundred meters north. It doesn't make any sense. It's as if whatever made these tracks just appeared from the sky."

"That is a possibility. Hopefully, the analysis of the soil will give an indication to the type of being that left these marks. Until we find out, TESSA would be foolish to attempt to mine this planet. The potential for danger is too great, in my estimation. Let's get back to the shuttle and the others."

They trudged through the mud the way they had come, walking in their own footprints to avoid sinking further into the mire. The putrid wind increased in force and the sky grew ever darker. Just as the NX1 shuttlecraft was in view, a voice came over the chief's COMlink.

"Chief Mack, come in Chief. Caffey reporting."

"Copy, Lieutenant," Mack replied.

"Sir, we found something you must see. Commander Roberts is on his way. Our location is thirty meters southwest of the shuttle landing. Over."

"We're on our way, Lt. Caffey. Mack out."

Ward took out her scancorder from her instrument transport case and locked in on Caffey's location.

"This way, Chief," she said, as she lead them around the shuttle and down another maze-like path. It was difficult to run on the marshy terrain, but the urgency of Caffey's communication pressed them on. Chief Mack spotted Commander Roberts and Lieutenants Giler and Caffey in a huddle near the wall of rotting vegetation. Caffey was covered from head to toe in the grayish-brown muck that made up the surface of the planet.

"What's going on?" asked the chief.

The crew stepped back to make room in the circle for the newcomers.

"Sir, I was on my way back from my inspection of the south quadrant," Caffey explained, "when I took a header into the mud. That's when I found it. If I weren't so damn clumsy, I would have walked right past it."

"What is it?" asked Ensign Ward.

"My scancorder read-out says that its organic compound is human," observed Lt. Giler, "but it looks like no human I've ever seen. And there are no signs of life. Whatever it is, it's dead."

"What would a human be doing on an uncharted planet?" Commander Roberts wondered aloud. "We are six light years from the nearest inhabited outpost and we've had no indication there are any other life forms in the area."

The chief knelt down to get a closer look at the specimen. Whatever it was, it had been charred beyond recognition. It was about one meter long and did, indeed, have a resemblance to the shape and size of a human child of about eight years old. Mack took out his protective gloves from his transport case and put them on. Gently, he scraped away the mud covering the mysterious discovery. He carefully turned it over and, from the shock of what he saw, recoiled onto his posterior into the muck.

"Oh, my god!"

Gasps came up from the huddled crew. Giler doubled over with nausea. Ward and Roberts stood transfixed. The seconds that followed seemed like hours as the crew attempted to absorb what they saw. On the ground before them was indeed a human child, or at least was once.

The exterior of the corpse was charred black, skin fused to bone, the face locked in an expression of agony. One eye was partially open and the nose was missing, exposing the nasal cavity; the mouth was frozen in a scream. Protruding from the chest near the collarbone grew three long tentacles that appeared to be made of flesh, muscle and ligament. Three more grew from the back. The legs and arms sprawled away from the torso; the exposed feet were toeless, yet possessed of cleat-like spikes on the bottoms.

Caffey was the first to speak.

"Sir, what should we do?"

Commander Roberts reached down, extending a gloved hand to Chief Mack, pulling him up from the mire. "Win, this is certainly not what we were expecting to find on a routine mining survey."

"Indeed, Seth." The chief paused, contemplating a plan of action. The others waited, afraid to move. "Whatever did this could still be around. We must be on highest alert. Giler, contact Fergus and Martinez. Ask them to bring a containment crate from the shuttle. We will take this discovery with us, and, hopefully, Lt. Martinez, with the aid of Dr. Mutara can make some sense of it."

"Sir," Lt. Caffey said, as she knelt next to the body, "my scancorder is detecting a sonic transmission. Its frequency is too low for us to hear, but it is getting progressively stronger."

Commander Roberts' COMlink emitted a high-pitched siren.

"The emergency alarm!" He pulled his COMlink from his transport case and responded. "Roberts here, over."

"Commander! Help!"

It was Ensign Morse, who had been sent to monitor the west quadrant. His voice was distorted by a low hum that buzzed like a swarm of insects.

"Morse, what's your location?" The commander pleaded.

"I am...one kilometer west southwest of the shuttle...sir, come quickly. I don't think I can fight it off alone."

"We're on our way. Roberts out. Caffey, Giler, let's roll. Chief, we need all the help we can get."

"I'm with you. Ward, wait for the others and meet us at the shuttle with the specimen."

"Yes, sir. Let us know if you need back-up," Ensign Ward offered.

Mack, Roberts, Caffey and Giler waded their way through the marsh as quickly as the terrain would allow. As they neared Morse's location, the low buzz they first heard over the COMlink grew louder. A blood-curdling scream froze them in their tracks.

"Morse!" yelled Lt. Caffey, as she ran toward the sound. The men followed closely, all the while slipping and lurching through the muddy, darkening marshland. None of them were prepared for the terror that awaited them around the stand of hedges.

An intense blue glow crept around the edge and over the top of the tall, rotting plant wall. The buzzing sound was nearly deafening. Like a giant swarm of insects with a core of blue fire, the being rose up above the heads of the OutStar crew. Six long silvery tentacles whipped the air, cracking and snapping. The surface below was scorched and smoldering; the smell of sulfur and burning metal permeated the atmosphere. Morse's body lay in an oval depression, charred black to the bone.

Chief Mack and his crew drew their proton pistols and fired on the creature, their blasts aimed at the blazing blue core. With each shot, the luminous heart of the creature pulsated and expanded.

"Sir, the shots seem to be strengthening the creature!" Commander Roberts shouted above the roar of the cloud-like monster. He took out his scancorder. "The core has increased from three meters to six meters. We are fueling it with every blast!"

"Cease fire!" Mack shouted. "Everyone get to the shuttle as quickly as possible."

Caffey and Giler ran to Morse's scorched remains and unceremoniously picked up his charred body. The monster loomed overhead, tentacles lashing out at the security specialists.

"Leave him!" ordered Chief Mack. "There is nothing we can do for him now. Save yourselves!"

"But sir, we can't leave him behind!" Giler protested. He and Caffey ignored the chief's directive and hoisted Morse's crumbling body upon their shoulders. The creature lowered its position, closing in on the friends. Struggling through the mud with their cumbersome cargo, the lieutenants moved slowly. Roberts urged them on.

"Come on, it's not safe! We have to get out of here!"

As they ran from the beast, Chief Mack used his COMlink to warn the rest of his team.

"Attention OutStar crew. Report immediately to NX1. I repeat, report immediately to NX1 for departure!"

A sweeping tentacle made contact with the ground just to the right of Giler and Caffey, another to the left. Before they could react, all six tentacles adhered to the sticky ground and the two were caught like animals in a cage, the blue core burning just over their heads. Chief Mack fired once more at the creature, hoping to dislodge one of the tentacles, but to no avail.

"Caffey! Giler! No!" wailed Commander Roberts.

The smoke-like creature lowered itself down on top of the two crewmembers and their departed friend; their desperate screams were obscured by the deafening hum of the creature. A wave of heat, like a tsunami, blew Mack and Roberts backward into the mud. The smell of metallic sulfur surged through the air. The leaders could only watch as their crew burned to death.

The creature arose from the ground, leaving behind the lifeless, blackened bodies of Giler, Caffey and Morse, as well as an oval imprint surrounded by tentacle marks in the sludge. Mack and Roberts scrambled to their feet as quickly as they could and ran in the direction of their shuttlecraft. A transmission came across Chief Mack's COMlink.

"Chief, we are being pursued by two clouds of smoke with glowing blue centers and long silvery tentacles!" Martinez reported.

"Martinez, whatever you do, do not fire. It will only make them bigger."

Commander Roberts drew his scancorder.

"Chief, I've locked on to their position."

"Martinez, we are on our way. Do your best to make it to the shuttle. Our only chance of survival is to get off this planet! Mack out."

Roberts and Mack continued their race for the shuttlecraft, as the smoke creature pursued, whipping its tentacles through the air, striking the ground close behind them. The beeping of the scancorder location tracker grew stronger. It was nearly dark as the NX1 came into view. Mack and Roberts switched on the lamps on their transport cases to light the path.

"If only there was a way to debilitate this thing until we can get away," Roberts panted, as he thought aloud. "The blasts from the proton pistols fed it, but…what if it got too much power. Maybe it would overload."

"Seth, I'm willing to try it. It may be our only chance," Mack agreed. "If we can just make it to the ship, we can use the proton canon."

They could see the science team in the distance coming from the south quadrant toward the shuttlecraft, as Mack and Roberts approached. Lieutenants Navalus and Fergus lead the team, instrument transport cases lighting the way. Lieutenant Martinez and Ensign Ward followed, carrying the containment crate with the remains of the mysterious mutant child. Two smoke-cloud creatures hovered ominously overhead in pursuit.

Chief Mack pulled his remote command cell from his case to open the shuttlecraft door and begin the engine commencement sequence. From his COMlink, he instructed his frightened crew.

"Seth, get into the shuttle and prepare the proton canon. Ensign Ward, get that crate into the shuttle. Everyone else, on my command, we will all fire our proton pistols at one creature and, maybe, just maybe, we can overpower it. If we can at least stun them, we should have a chance to escape."

Roberts ran up the ramp of the NX1 and into the command center. He quickly began the canon activation sequence and waited for the chief's signal. Ward took the crate from Martinez and continued, struggling with the weight alone. Mack and the others crouched into firing position.

"On three. One…two…three!"

The team fired on the creature closest to them—the one that had taken Giler, Morse and Caffey. It was nearly overhead as they crouched about forty meters from the shuttle. The force of the synchronized blasts caused the creature to freeze in mid-air for a fraction of a second. A surge of blue light burst from the center of the being raining down a shower of glowing sparks onto the team, searing their skin.

They screamed in pain, the hot particles burning through their flight jackets. The cloud particles dispersed into the air, as each tentacle burned out like a lighted fuse.

"Run for the shuttle!" shouted Mack, then asking into the COMlink, "Seth, is the canon ready?"

"Ready, Chief! I've got you on screen."

Another scream went up from behind them. Ensign Ward was struggling with the containment crate when one of the two remaining cloud-creatures lashed out at her, knocking her to the ground. The snap of the tendril across her back sliced through her flight jacket cutting into her skin.

"Aaagh!" Ensign Ward cried, as she tried to regain her footing.

"Seth, one of them has Sarah. Fire now!"

The creature's tentacles reached for Ward, one wrapping around her left ankle, another around her right thigh. The monster raised her off the ground dangling her ten to fifteen meters in the air. The blast from the proton canon caused the core of the beast to explode, once again, raining blue fire.

Ward fell with a thud to the ground. Lt. Navalus ran to her side.

"Sir, she's not breathing, but she's still alive."

Before anyone could make a move, one of the two remaining smoke-creatures dove in for an attack, leaving a trail of smoke in its wake. Martinez grabbed the containment crate and dashed for the shuttle. Fergus reflexively fired his pistol at the charging force and ran to help Ward. The core of the monster expanded and the heat surrounding it intensified.

"Fergus, hold your fire!" the chief commanded. "Seth, fire the canon!"

With no other means of resuscitation at his disposal, Navalus attempted CPR on an unresponsive Ensign Ward. The beam of the proton canon narrowly missed its moving target, as the cloud of fire continued its descent, landing squarely on the fallen researcher and her rescuers. A second blast from the canon hit its target with a thunderous explosion, but too late. Lt. Martinez made it to the shuttle ramp just in time to see her protégé and colleagues engulfed by the flaming blue of the creature.

As Chief Mack ran for the NX1, he activated the departure sequence with his command cell. One more death-swarm loomed overhead. Inside the shuttle,

Commander Roberts took the controls and initiated lift-off. Mack leaped for the edge of the ramp as it rose from the surface of UC-788. He crawled his way into the shuttle just the vertical thrusters ignited and the NX1 burst into the air. Martinez, still reeling from their narrow escape, walked stoically to the proton canon and fired. A grim smile crossed her lips as she watched from the viewscreen the blue firebrand pouring from the sky.

2

Visions of Terror

Captain Jack A. Jones sat in the command center of OutStar One, impatiently waiting for word from the research detail dispatched to the Alterian system. Venturing into uncharted space was always unsettling, even for experienced survey crews. He ran his fingers through his thick, wavy, dirty blond hair, rested his chin on his fist and his elbow on the armrest of his console chair. Jones' long legs stretched out before him creating an obstacle for Lieutenant Commander Anjum Sarwar to walk around.

Lt. Com. Sarwar took his seat to the captain's right at the pilot's console. He smoothed his dark goatee, took a deep breath and let out an audible sigh. Considerably shorter than the captain, Sarwar's feet just met the floor under his chair. He shifted until he found a comfortable position, pushed up his square black-framed glasses on his nose and called up the communication log on his monitor.

"Captain, perhaps we should try to make contact with the shuttle again. Communication to the Alterian system can be unpredictable."

"We are of the same mind, Lieutenant. See if you can get them on their COMlinks."

"Yes, sir," Lt. Commander Sarwar replied. "OutStar One to Chief Mack. Chief Mack, please copy."

There was no response, only crackles and pops. Captain Jones got up and paced over to the viewscreen. The blackness of space extended before him, an endless expanse stretching out for eternity. Somewhere out there were his friends, the people who only recently were strangers, but who quickly, to his surprise, became like family.

A voice came over the starCOM.

"Chief Mack to OutStar One. OutStar One, do you copy?"

"Captain, it's them!" Lt. Sarwar exclaimed.

"OutStar One Command, Lieutenant Commander Anjum Sarwar, over."

"Anjum, I...barely hear..." the Chief replied.

"Sir, give us your location. I'm losing communication."

"Lieutenant, turn...voice-text translat...." Lt. Sarwar punched the translator code into the computer and the words of Chief Mack appeared on the monitor. Captain Jones walked around behind Lt. Commander Sarwar, put his hands on the back of the pilot's chair and looked over his shoulder at the monitor. We have landed safely on the target planet, referred to hereinafter as UC-788. We are about to begin our exploration, but the light is not with us. We may need to be here an extra day. Alert Captain Roberts and TESSA. I will contact you again when we are ready to depart. Mack out.

"Well, Captain. They arrived safely," Sarwar reported.

"Excellent. That is good news." Captain Jones took his seat.

"Captain, what about our position?" Sarwar asked. "We are approaching the Venga system and should arrive at the TESSA outpost in 96 hours. It could be a problem if they aren't back in time."

"Stay the course. We'll wait for word from Mack and Roberts before we make any decisions. If they are able to complete the mission by tomorrow, we should be able to report to TESSA on time."

Lieutenant Tapia Tunica came through the transparent sliding doors of the command center. She did not wear the OutStar uniform, but a cream colored Mandarin-style pantsuit that complimented her warm, terra cotta skin. Her long, straight black hair was twisted into plaits that looped intricately around the base of her skull and, if released from the ornate gold clasps, would fall well past her slim waist. She seemed to glide when she walked, her steps always silent; some called her sneaky, others mysterious. Tapia possessed an intuition and telepathic skill known throughout the star system and her shockingly green eyes exuded compassion for all beings.

"Captain, I am sorry to interrupt, but I must speak with you immediately."

"Lt. Tunica, please come in." Jones welcomed, rising to greet her. He extended his hand and she took it. "What is on your mind?"

"Sir, I was just visited by a vision that was most disturbing. Has Chief Mack reported to you?"

"Only briefly to say they have arrived. Communication is difficult to maintain in the Alterian system."

"I see," Lt. Tunica nodded. "Captain, I must say, I fear the worst for this crew. My vision, though not completely lucid, indicated great trouble."

"Please, Lieutenant, sit down and continue. You have my full attention." Captain Jones indicated a swiveling chair to the left of his own. The two officers sat. Lt. Commander Sarwar leaned in with fascination.

"Well, sir, I was meditating on the sacred cloth of my ancestors when I went into a trance. I could see only a smoky haze at first, but then it became clearer; the haze had a form. A swarm of tiny creatures, insects perhaps, hovered around a luminous blue sphere. Fire shot down from the center of the sphere, leaving a scorched path in its wake. Then a silver cord dropped from the sphere, wrapped around a human form and pulled the being into the sphere, engulfing it with blue light. With a flash, the trance was broken."

Lt. Tunica leaned back in her seat, nearly as exhausted from the retelling as she was from receiving the vision. She closed her eyes and took a deep breath. Jones and Sarwar were speechless for moment. The captain took her hand and patted it gently.

"Tapia," he whispered. "Are you all right? Should I call Dr. Mutara?"

"Yes...No, I'm fine, but yes, please call her. I fear there will be casualties."

"What makes you think this vision is related to our research team?" Sarwar asked.

"When I recovered my presence, I stood in the center of my room and walked to the door. As I opened it, I felt a sharp pain in my abdomen and I saw the face of Ensign Sarah Ward, the young botanist that joined us last week. I can't explain it logically, but I fear the worst."

"Thank you for bringing this to my attention, Lieutenant. You have my assurance that I will take your warning seriously and do what I can to prevent a disaster. Anjum, attempt a communication with Chief Mack. If it fails, try Commander Roberts and on down the line. Keep trying until you get through."

"Yes, sir," the Lieutenant Commander acquiesced.

"Lt. Tunica, please let me know if you learn anything else."

"Yes, Captain. I certainly will. If you will excuse me, sir, I will let you get back to your duties and I will return to mine."

"Of course, Lieutenant. Thank you again for the warning."

"You are welcome, Captain."

The colleagues shook hands. Lt. Tunica turned and glided through the door.

Captain Jones returned to his command console, punched in the code for Dr. Mutara, leaned his head back and waited.

****

DOCTOR ODETTE MUTARA stepped through the doorway of the bridge and the doors closed behind her. A buxom woman, she was simply dressed, as always, in an eggplant-colored sweater, black pants and a black lab coat. Her hair was closely cropped and, though, she dressed most plainly, she wore a dazzling gold choker around her ebony throat. Dr. Mutara was petite, yet her presence was commanding. She looked around curiously and smiled when her eyes found the captain.

"Hello, Captain. I came as soon as I could. I am not often summoned to central command," she said. Her warm smile was friendly and comforting.

Jones was startled awake by her voice. He jumped up to his feet and walked briskly to greet her.

"Ah, Doctor Mutara. Thank you for coming. Your presence is always welcomed, whether you are summoned or not. Let's sit down for a moment, shall we?"

"Thank you." Dr. Mutara sat in the swiveling chair Lt. Tunica vacated minutes before. The captain took his seat and turned to face the doctor.

"Tapia has had a vision. She foresees danger for the research team in Alteria, and I would like us to prepare for the worst. Excuse me a moment." The captain turned to Sarwar. "Any communication with NX1?"

"Not yet, sir. I've tried each member of the team individually and the shuttlecraft itself. I have gotten no response. I set the computer to keep trying until we make communication."

"Good work, Anjum." Jones turned back to Dr. Mutara. "Dr. Mutara, have you had any experience in this situation before? I have always trusted Tapia's gift, but I don't want to overreact."

"Hope for the best, prepare for the worst. That is always a safe policy, Captain. I will set up an emergency triage in the medical center and have technicians standing by. Do you have an ETA on the team?"

"We expect them in two to three days. They were to begin their return at the end of the day, but it seems they will not be able to conclude until tomorrow."

"I will begin preparations immediately. Thank you for alerting me to the situation. If you have any more news, please send it my way at once. In case you were wondering, Captain, my personal faith in Tapia's gift is strong. You are right to take it seriously."

"Thank you, Doctor. I'll keep you apprised of any occurrences." The pair shook hands and held one another's gaze for a moment. Jones was the first to look away.

"Thank you, Captain." Mutara smiled and took her leave.

3

The Return

THE SURVIVORS OF THE ATTACK on the OutStar One crew sat in silence on the command deck of the NX1 shuttlecraft. The bright lights contradicted the gloom that hung over the three officers. Chief Mack leaned back in his reclining command chair, his eyes closed, his face toward the ceiling. His lean, muscular body was wracked with pain from the scorching sparks of the exploding creatures. The sores left behind on his smooth mocha skin oozed with blood and puss. Commander Roberts sat next to the chief with his head in his hands, elbows on his knees, his shaggy blonde hair hanging over his eyes while the events of the previous hour replayed in his mind as if on a loop. Lieutenant Jessica Martinez stood staring blankly out of the viewscreen, her small hands still on the proton canon from which she fired the fatal blow to the last of the cloud creatures.

"Seth," Chief Mack broke the silence. "See if you can get OutStar on the starCOM."

Commander Roberts looked up from the floor, put his hands on the tops of his thighs and rose from his hunched position. He walked over to the navigational control panel and punched in the contact code for OutStar One. Exhausted, he sank down onto the padded stool in front of the console.

"They are not responding. Judging from their location, we should meet up with them about a day from the TESSA outpost in the Venga system. That puts us at about two days from rendezvous."

"Damn. I don't want to surprise them with this news, but we are going to need all the rest we can get for the inquiry when we return. Configure the viewCOM to record a message and program it to attempt connection with OS One every sixty seconds. Then lock us in to their position and activate autopilot. I plan to take advantage of the cryo-sleep chambers and I suggest the two of you do the same." Chief Mack stood slowly, stretched his arms above his head and rubbed his weatherworn face and closely-cropped black hair with his hands. He walked over to Lt. Martinez, who still stood frozen by the canon, and put his large calloused hands on her narrow shoulders.

"Come on, Jess. Go get some sleep."

"OK, Win," she finally said. "I'll just log the specimens we managed to save."

"The log can wait. Seth, is the viewCOM ready to record?'

"Not yet, Win." Commander Roberts paused and noticed the burns on the chief's body. "Don't you want something for your back? You look like you were attacked by monsters. Oh, wait. You were."

"In cryo-sleep, all body functions are suspended. I'll be the same coming out as going in. When we get back to OS One, Dr. Mutara can have a look."

"Okay, you're the boss," Commander Roberts replied. "You're all set to prepare the statement."

"Thanks, Seth. Take Jess and get some rest. I'll finish up here and join you shortly."

"Okay. Come on, Jess, let's get suspended."

The two officers walked through the door of the command deck, down a narrow, but brightly lit corridor to the transport shaft. The door opened at their approach and they stepped into the compartment. Martinez pushed in the code for the third sub-floor, the door closed and, in an instant, they were three levels below the deck. The door opened and Martinez and Roberts slowly walked through the passageway to a large glass-enclosed room. Through the glass door were six horizontal chrome cylinders on platforms, each with a door of its own. A keypad located to the right of each door allowed the user to determine the length of sleep required, as well as level of suspension. For longer journeys, of perhaps two or three months, full suspension would be preferable. For a shorter journey, such as the two-day trip back to OutStar One, only a partial suspension would be necessary, allowing for an easier and shorter re-acclimation process.

Roberts entered 42 hours into his chamber data bank and indicated 65% suspension of animation. Martinez followed suit. The doors of the chambers opened and the two friends each stepped into their own. The doors closed around them and the sound of hissing gas filled the room. As the cryo-gas pumped in, the beleaguered explorers were swept into a two-day sleep.

****

THE NX-1 SHUTTLECRAFT reached the outer rim of the Vengan solar system on schedule and fired its forward braking thrusters slowing the ship from star drive into sub-star drive. The cryo-chamber computer revived the three officers and opened the chamber doors.

As they awoke, trying to shake off the effects of the cryo-gas, the remaining NX1 crew was bombarded by the amber flashing lights and screeching sound of the proximity sensors that told them they had reached the border of their destined solar system. Seth could barely open his watery blue eyes as he climbed out of the cryo-cylinder.

"Wingate, you were right. I still feel as awful as when I went in there," he complained.

"I'm just glad we are almost home," Chief Mack replied, walking through the glass doors of the cryo-center and over to a control pad on the opposite wall. He punched in the alarm-disabling sequence, giving them silence.

"Gentlemen," Lt. Martinez greeted her colleagues, holding her head and looking as ashen as she did two days before. Her long dark brown hair was a mess of curls and knots. Her warm brown eyes were bloodshot and bleary.

"Good morning, Jess," Seth said, giving her a pat on the shoulder. "You look as terrible as I feel."

"Thanks, Seth. You know how to start a girl's day off on the right foot," she laughed half-heartedly.

"Well, guys," Wingate said, "let's get ourselves cleaned up and ready to face the rest of the OutStar One crew. It's going to be a rough day. I'll meet you on the bridge at 15:00 hours."

4

The Worst

Dr. Mutara sat in her comfortable quarters reading an ancient medical book from her ancestral homeland of Botswana, Africa. She surrounded herself with soft light and cozy fabrics. Though she appeared plain on the outside, the good doctor enjoyed the finer things. Odette was a sixth generation doctor and learned much about the art of medicine from her mother and the women of her family who preceded her. She was very proud of this history, but was never vain or boastful. She appreciated all she had and took nothing for granted.

A knock at her door interrupted her studies.

"Come in," she called, pushing the remote access pad on the end table next to her. Captain Jack Jones poked his head through the opening door.

"Dr. Mutara, I am sorry to bother you in your private chamber, but I have urgent and devastating news."

"What is it, sir?" she asked, putting the book on the end table.

"We've received, at long last, a communiqué from NX1. It seems that the research team was indeed attacked by a creature very close to the one Tapia described."

"No!" she shook her head forcefully. She looked up at the captain and caught his gaze. She patted the space next to her on the comfortable lounger. "Jack, please sit down. You must be exhausted." He sat next to her, taking care not to make physical contact with her.

"Thank you, yes. I am quite beside myself."

"Please, tell me what has happened." She patted the hand that rested on his right knee. He drew in a sharp breath, but soon relaxed at the calming touch of her warm hand.

"Only three survived. Three out of nine, Odette." He looked at the floor, unable to look into her eyes. "Apparently, their pistols were no match for this creature and before they could escape to the shuttle, six of them were burned alive."

"This is horrifying news. Who, may I ask, were the survivors?"

"Wingate, Seth and Jessica. Tapia was right. Ensign Ward was among the casualties."

"Are there injuries among the living?"

"Wingate looked as if someone poured acid on him. I don't know if Jessica or Seth were hurt; Wingate didn't mention it. What he did mention, however, was the discovery of a corpse of a mutant human child with tentacles and spikes on its feet."

"What?"

"That is why I've come to you. We must figure out how this child came to be mutated on such a remote planet in the mostly uncharted Alterian star system. The sooner we are able to report to TESSA, the sooner things can get back to normal."

"Of course, sir. Will our wounded warriors be arriving soon?"

"We expect them in about six hours."

"I will be ready for them. And Jack," she took his hand in hers and looked deeply into his sparkling, but saddened green eyes, "if there is anything else I can do to help you, I will. You merely have to ask."

****

THE NX1 ENTERED the Vengan system and made its final approach to OutStar One. Commander Roberts was at the command panel when a member of the docking crew appeared on their viewscreen.

"Commander, would you like to dock manually or use the automatic beacon? The docking doors are activated and ready, sir."

"We will bring it in on manual," Seth said. He carefully guided the NX1 into OutStar One's landing bay and lowered the ship onto its landing pad. He shut down the shuttlecraft's engines and waited for pressure equalization to be achieved.

"We're home, kids," Seth joked, in an attempt to lighten the ever-darkening mood. None of the three remaining crewmembers wanted to face the reality of what they experienced in Alteria. The prospect of saying it out loud before an inquiry board, let alone their fellow crewmates, was troubling and they all feared the impending interrogation.

The green pressure signal-light blinked and Seth pushed the button that lowered the ramp and opened the door of the shuttle. Chief Mack and Commander Roberts looked out from the entrance, each carrying two containment bags of bio-samples. They were relieved to be back in the familiar surroundings of the OutStar, but apprehensive about their reception. Would they be blamed for the deaths of their friends and crewmembers or would people understand that every possible attempt was made to save their fallen comrades? Lt. Martinez walked out behind them carrying the crate containing their dark discovery.

They reached the bottom of the ramp and passed through the sliding doors that lead from the bay into the ship's reception chamber. They were greeted by the strained, yet smiling faces of Dr. Mutara, Captain Jones, Lt. Tunica and two medical technicians.

"Welcome home, friends," the captain said, extending his hand to shake those of his colleagues. "We have been anxiously awaiting you."

"Thank you, Captain. Doctor, Lieutenant, thank you for coming to meet us. We have had a rough journey and it is nice to see friendly faces," Chief Mack replied. "I'm sure you have many questions, but..."

"That can wait," Dr. Mutara interrupted. "First, you all must report to the medical center for complete analysis. Your health is paramount at this stage. I'm sure our curiosities will be satisfied in due time."

"Yes, Doctor, you are absolutely right," the captain agreed.

"Chief Mack, if there is any way I can be of assistance to the three of you in your transition after this tragedy, please let me know." Lt. Tunica offered.

"Thank you, Tapia. I think we should follow doctor's orders and get ourselves to med-bay at once." The two medical technicians relieved Lt.

Martinez of her containment crate and the men of their bags. Chief Mack indicated for his crew to exit the reception chamber. "Doctor, the containment bags should be taken to the bio-lab for immediate analysis of the planet's soil and core compositions. The crate, however, well… I would like you to handle it personally."

"Of course, Chief, I would be happy to. Ensign, take the crate to my lab immediately. I will begin as soon as you've had a thorough going-over." She smiled again at the chief and his crew. "You'll be good as new in no time."

****

THE DOCTOR PACED back and forth across her examination room. Chief Mack sat on a cold metal table, the upper portion of his torso bare to the waist and his blue undershirt in his hand. The large burns on his back and shoulders were bandaged with regenerative skin replacement patches.

"I'll make out the death codes for each one and notify the next of kin," Dr. Mutara said in a somber voice. "Wingate, you have been through a terrible ordeal. I want you to rest and regain your strength. Once TESSA is notified, they will surely launch a full inquiry and you and your team will need to be at your best."

"Yes, Doctor. How are Seth and Jessica?"

"As well as can be expected. They have some of the same burns you have, but not to the same degree. Their mental states are another question altogether. Seth was cracking jokes, as usual, but Jessica was oddly silent. I've never known her to be so withdrawn. I have recommend meeting with Tapia and hope that will be of some help to both of them. It wouldn't hurt you either."

"We'll see, Doctor," he replied skeptically.

"Well, if I may take my leave of you sir, I would like to begin the autopsy of the mutant child as soon as possible." Dr. Mutara turned her back to the chief and washed her hands in the sink opposite the exam table as he put on his shirt and zipped his flight jacket. "Wingate. Please get some rest."

"I'll try, Doctor, I'll try," he said, unconvincingly. He hopped down off the exam table. "And thanks."

Dr. Mutara turned around and watched Chief Mack exit the med-bay. It was time to begin the dreaded, but fascinating task at hand. She walked over to the control panel near the door of the brightly lit exam room and punched the code for the lab. A voice came through the voiceCOM.

"Med-lab One, Ensign Yang."

"Ensign, I am on my way. Please make final preparations for the specimen autopsy."

"Everything is ready and awaiting your arrival, Doctor."

"Thank you. Mutara out."

****

COMMANDER ROBERTS AND Lieutenant Martinez, wearing their maroon dress uniforms—tailored pants and short jackets with the OS One logo embroidered on the breast pocket—joined Chief Mack on his way to the main conference room just off the bridge of OutStar One. The three walked in silence as they passed curious, staring crewmembers. Word had gotten around, in the day and a half since their return, of the terrible tragedy of UC-788, and the entire OutStar crew was in mourning for the six lost explorers.

"How you, feeling, Chief?" Seth asked with a false cheerfulness. "I, for one, feel good as new. It's amazing what a nap can do."

Wingate smiled wanly. "Let's keep the sarcasm to a minimum, shall we. TESSA is unlikely to find any of this amusing."

"Forget it… sir," snapped Roberts.

"Seth, we're all on edge. Let's just try to get through this, okay," pleaded Lt. Martinez.

Seth reached out and squeezed her hand, giving her a comforting wink. The three paused outside the door, which opened at their approach, looked at each other, took a deep collective breath and walked through it.

****

Sitting around a large, oval-shaped, chrome and glass table were Captain Jones, Lt. Tunica and Dr. Mutara; the captain had also summoned Commander & Chief Vincent Jones of Galactic Command, Captain Leo J. Chance and, via viewCOM, TESSA President Nariko Fema. They all rose to their feet as the Chief Operations Officer of OutStar One entered with his security expert and top biologist.

"Thank you all for coming on such short notice," Chief Mack began, sitting at the head of the table, motioning for the others to be seated as well. "As you know this is a matter of great urgency and the cooperation of all will be required if anything is to be done about it. I assume Captain Jones has briefed you on the details of our mission." There were nods among the assembled dignitaries. "Then I think we should begin with the autopsy report of Dr. Mutara, if no one objects. We will then answer any of your questions. Doctor, you have the floor."

"Thank you, Chief Mack." Dr. Mutara stood and stepped to a slim glass podium equipped with a viewCOM and data read-out monitor. She punched in her access code on the keypad and photos of the autopsied specimen appeared on the viewscreen behind her. "While my findings are inconclusive, as there is no previous record of an occurrence such as this, I have determined several things to be fact. One, the specimen retrieved by Chief Mack and his crew, is indeed of human origin. From its teeth and bone fragments, we have determined that it is male, about eight years of age at the time of death. If you will notice in the pictures, three tentacles, which are indeed made of human tissue—muscle and ligament—are attached to its clavicle across the front of the body and three to its shoulder blades and spine across the back. It is unclear, because of the state of decay, whether the tentacles were surgically attached or bred into the genetic make-up of the boy. More tests will need to be done to make that determination." Dr. Mutara paused and took a drink of water from the glass on her podium.

"Doctor," Captain Chance asked, "What about the spikes on the feet?"

"Yes, well, the same mystery surrounds the spikes, although because they are made of metal, a chromium-platinum alloy, it is my assumption that they were embedded into the child's feet with surgery. Even with the state of genetic engineering that exists, it is nearly impossible to grow non-living tissue from living tissue."

"How do you suppose this child came to be on UC-788?" asked President Fema.

"Well, Madame President, it is my belief from examination of the soil samples taken from the planet, that at one time there were many of these mutant-children on UC-788. Perhaps this one was left behind after an evacuation, or more likely, it tried to escape. It was killed in the same manner as the unfortunate OutStar One researchers—burned to the bone by the cloud-swarm creature described by the survivors and recorded on their scancorders."

"Is there any indication as to where they came from in the first place?" Commander & Chief Jones wondered.

"Not at this time, sir. That is the greater part of the mystery and why we've asked you here. Chief Mack, I have nothing further. Would you like to take over from here?"

"Yes, thank you, Dr. Mutara." Chief Mack rose and walked to the podium as Dr. Mutara returned to her seat. "To answer your question, Commander & Chief, we have not yet made any determinations as to the origin of this being. It is our hope that further examination of the soil and vegetation samples will give us some clue as to the make-up and origin of the creatures that attacked us. Lt. Martinez is our best forensic pathologist. Her analysis will hopefully shed more light on the mystery."

"Lieutenant, do you have any leads at this time?" Captain Chance ventured.

"The only thing we've determined at this stage, sir, is that the being is a silicon-based life form," Martinez explained. "We were able to take tissue samples from Chief Mack and Commander Roberts, who were burned by two of the creatures when they exploded upon us, which contained organic matter we believe to be derivative of the attacker."

"Are there any more questions?" Chief Mack asked the assembled.

"Yes, Chief Mack, I have one more question," said Captain Chance. "How do we know this is not some kind of publicity stunt to promote your survey business? You've shown us pictures and reports, but where is the evidence that corroborates your story?"

Chief Mack gripped the podium tightly and took a deep breath, staring at Chance in disbelief.

"With all due respect, sir, how dare you question the validity of our report? We lost six valuable crewmembers and dear friends in this attack. What more do you want?"

"All I am asking, Mr. Mack, is 'how do we know you aren't just trying to cover up some failure in leadership?' No being of this kind has ever been seen before. Why now? Why on your watch?"

"I take full responsibility for my crew. If you would like to file charges against me, please feel free.

But we were attacked and my colleagues died in the pursuit of knowledge—hired by your governing body for your benefit and advancement. Perhaps you would like to take some responsibility for the safety of those in this universe that your military serves. How did this monster appear under your radar, sir?"

Lt. Tunica stood and raised her hands in the air.

"Gentlemen, please. This is not the time for accusations or casting blame. We have a problem here that affects all of us. We need to work together in order to protect ourselves and our children. If we give in to in-fighting and name-calling, we are useless to one another. Perhaps our distinguished guests from Galactic Command would like a tour of the med-bay to see the evidence for themselves."

"Thank you, Lt. Tunica," Captain Jones intoned. "Well spoken and a wonderful suggestion. Dr. Mutara, would you escort our guests to the medical center?"

"Of course, Captain." Dr. Mutara rose and walked toward the door of the conference room. "Gentlemen, please follow me. Madame President, we will arrange for a viewscreen in the examination lab so you may participate in our little tour as well."

"Thank you, Doctor," President Fema replied. "Perhaps I'll have a word with Chief Mack and his crew in the meantime."

"Of course, Madame President," Chief Mack said humbly.

Dr. Mutara escorted Commander & Chief Jones and Captain Chance from the bridge to the medical center. Chief Mack took his seat at the conference table and faced President Fema on the viewscreen. She spoke first.

"Chief Mack, please know that you have our deepest condolences and sympathies on the loss of your colleagues in this horrible tragedy. The Established Stellar Systems Alliance will do all it can to aid in the investigation and come to a speedy resolution. It behooves us to work together in this situation. Also know that it is Captain Chance's job to be skeptical and demand substantial evidence in matters such as these. I'm sure no disrespect was intended. While I don't condone the way he handled the situation, I do feel he was within his rights to question you."

"I understand, Madame President. Thank you for your concern and for taking the time out of your busy schedule to join us today. I apologize for my outburst. Tensions are running high, but there is no excuse for my behavior."

"On the contrary, you reacted as many of us would under the circumstances."

The voice of a lab technician came over the voiceCOM.

"Captain, Dr. Mutara is ready for President Fema to join us in examination lab three."

"Thank you. Madame President, I will switch you over to Dr. Mutara. We appreciate your assurance that TESSA will be fair in its investigation. We intend to cooperate fully and in any capacity you require."

"We will be in contact with you soon, Chief Mack. Thank you for your diligence and hard work. Captain, Lieutenants, thank you for your cooperation and please accept my deepest condolences for your loss during this ordeal."

The viewscreen went black. The officers of OutStar One stared at one another for a moment. Commander Roberts broke the silence.

"I think that went well."

"Excuse me, Commander." Two security officers entered the room. "We have a security breach in the med-center computer lab. It seems someone tapped into the computer, downloaded and copied the autopsy report. The computer's log shows that the break-in occurred just before your meeting with Galactic Command started."

"Put the station on full alert immediately." The Commander jumped to his feet. "No one is to leave OutStar One until further notice and track any recently departed craft. Call all security personnel to the briefing center for further instructions."

5

Proof

NEAR CHALDEAN 5, IN THE Vengan system, a mysterious cloud was making its way toward the planet. What seemed to be lightning bolts shot from it, striking an orbiting weather satellite and destroying it. A supply ship lifted off from a port of the Chelsea colony's capitol city after delivering medical supplies. As the ship changed its vector and reached the stratosphere, it encountered the same strange cloud. With no way to avoid it, the ship penetrated the cloud, and the bolts of lightning struck the ship causing a breech in the hull.

Captain Erious Rea Fielding attempted to send a distress signal, but failed—all electrical energy had been drained, including emergency power. The ship started to break apart, large chunks of metal and debris exploded into the stratosphere. She called out to her partner and co-captain, but received no response. Liesel dan Poluondi lay dead in the passageway between the bridge and the cargo bay, blood oozing from her fractured skull. With nothing else to do, Captain Fielding hurried to the life pod and ejected from the wreckage just as the ship exploded in a huge fireball.

As the life pod descended into the atmosphere, Captain Fielding struggled to stabilize it, but she was not able to divert power to the braking thrusters. Moving quickly, she reached over and pulled the manual ejector release lever, catapulting herself out of the pod. The emergency capsule filled with anti-gravity gas, slowing her decent and allowing for a soft landing on the hot desert plain. She disengaged the door of the capsule and stepped outside noticing the strange cloud that had just destroyed her ship.

"My God, that thing is headed towards the Chelsea colony and there's nothing I can do to warn them."

She checked her scancorder and, to her surprise, it was still in working condition. She re-entered the pod and plugged the scancorder power pack into the

COMunit and ran a diagnostic test. The system was damaged beyond repair. She had no means of direct communication.

The scancorder indicated there were seventy-five kilometers of hot desert and mountainous terrain between her location and the colony. It was early afternoon and the Chaldean sun was beaming down hot, unforgiving rays. Rea knew that what little emergency water was in the pod would help her survive no more then a few days at the most.

She adjusted her scancorder to emit a low band distress beacon hoping that it would be picked up before the power pack died, leaving her stranded. She knew it would be foolish to venture away from the safety and shelter of the pod, but she also knew that soon it would be impossible to reenter the pod as the heat-buildup turned the interior into an oven.

****

"WE ARE PICKING up a distress call from the Chelsea colony on Chaldean 5," Lt. Sarwar announced via voiceCOM from the command center. "Captain, that colony is inhabited by children and supervisory adults who take care of them while their parents build the colony settlement."

"How many people are we talking about?" asked Lt. Martinez.

"Well, according settlement records, close to 4200, but possibly more," he replied.

"Put us on viewCOM with the colony now!" the chief demanded. A bleeding communication officer appeared on the screen.

"This is Communications Officer Lorell on Chaldean 5 in the Chelsea colony. We are under attack from some sort of…" He paused for a moment. Loud buzzing noises and screaming filled their ears. "Some sort of giant smoke creature that has split into several creatures. I don't know why, but they…they seem to be going primarily after the children."

"Can you give us a visual from your outside colony viewers?" Captain Jones asked.

"Yes, switching to outside colony viewers now."

The officers in the conference room gasped in horror as they saw an alien, similar to the one that attacked them on UC-788, lashing about, laying waste to the colony. The cloud creature had split into ten separate entities and was taking over the city. The crew of the OutStar could see in the public square, a group of six children attempting to escape the frightful creatures by ducking through a doorway and slamming the door shut behind them. The smoke-monsters blasted the door with a thunderous lightning flash, vaporizing it. The children screamed as the creature's long silvery tendrils wrapped around them, pulling them into the central core of the creature. The children seemed to vaporize; there were no remains, no charred corpses, they were just gone.

"Lt. Sarwar, contact Commander & Chief Vincent Jones and Captain Leo Chance in the med-bay and tell them to report immediately to the command center. We will meet them there."

"Yes, Captain."

****

"My god, Wingate, what's happening?" asked the C & C, observing the carnage on the command center viewscreen.

"It seems the Chelsea colony on Chaldean 5 is under attack by creatures eerily similar to the ones that attacked us on UC-788. Sarwar, bring back Officer Lorell."

"Yes, sir." The image reverted back to the communication station on the Chelsea colony.

"Officer Lorell, do you have any defensive capabilities?" asked the captain.

"Sir, our laser pistols seem to have no effect on these creatures," he said. Lorell looked around as a thunderous crashes continued in the background.

Suddenly, the screen image shook violently. One of the monsters burst through the wall of the COMstation. Lorell turned and opened fire while trying to dodge its stinging tendrils. He was not quick enough. The creature reached out with one of its many tentacles and grabbed Lorell, picked him up and held him for a few motionless seconds. The core of the creature suddenly became a fiery blue. The monster retracted its tentacle, pulling Lorell into flaming core. In an instant, blackened corpse dropped to the floor. The fire faded as the creature lashed out, destroying the COMstation, and severing all contact with the ravished colony. The assembly stared at the blank screen in horrified silence.

"Well, Captain, I don't know what further proof you need that the attack was real. You've seen it for yourself," Chief Mack said with a tinge of condescension in his voice. "I would advise an immediate dispatch to Chaldean 5 before you have an interstellar incident on your hands. One wouldn't want a failure in leadership to cost anymore lives."

"How dare you…" Chance began, before Commander & Chief Jones interrupted him.

"Point taken, Wingate. Chance, send the nearest battle cruiser immediately to Chaldean 5. We must stop these creatures before they destroy the whole galaxy."

Chance took his COMlink out of left breast pocket and stormed out of the command center. The C & C turned to Chief Mack and Captain Jones.

"Gentlemen, you have my apologies for Chance's behavior. I don't know what has come over him, but he has been acting very strangely as of late."

"Thank you, Commander & Chief," the Captain replied. "We better than anyone understand the stresses that come with working for Galactic Command. That's why we left."

"Of course, Jack. How could I forget?" Commander & Chief Jones nodded. Chance returned to the command center replacing his COMlink to his pocket.

"Excuse me Commander & Chief, I have just been informed by Galactic Command Base that there are no battle cruisers in the area of Chaldean 5. It will take days before our ships would reach the colony. It seems that OutStar One is the closest vessel to the colony at this time. This crew must mount a rescue operation under our aegis."

"Why should we help you now?" Chief Mack demanded. "Remember, we are just a civilian business entity trying to drum up publicity."

The Commander & Chief, again, intervened.

"Please, Wingate. We need you. You have the know-how and the resources—I never thought I'd say this, but when you and Jack left Galactic Command, I knew we were losing the best. Here's your chance to show us what we are really missing. And hey, who doesn't want to be a hero?"

6

The Rescue

DR. ODETTE MUTARA, AND HER medical staff, along with thirty other OutStar One personnel, assembled in the briefing arena to volunteer for the mission. The chief walked down the ramp into the arena with Captain Jack Jones, Commander Seth Roberts, Lt. Commander Anjum Sarwar, Lt. Tapia Tunica and Lt. Jessica Martinez to address the assembly. He stood with his arms behind him, his hands clasped and his face tight as he began to speak to his volunteer crew.

"Ladies and gentleman of OS One, I'm glad you are here. As some of you already know, we have been asked by Galactic Command to take on a rescue operation. We are the only ship in this quadrant with some capabilities of a battle cruiser, and being a scientific survey ship, we have a full hospital and research lab on board.

"There is an emergency situation on Chaldean 5, one of the outer-sector settlements. We do know there have been casualties, but how many is still a mystery. This will be a dangerous mission and you are not required by your employment with OutStar to participate. You will be adequately compensated, but you are under no obligation to enlist in this hazardous duty.

"The Chelsea colony is under attack by aliens very similar to those that attacked and killed the six OutStar scientists on UC-788. We are dealing with dangerous and unpredictable creatures. If any of you would like to reconsider your part in this mission, now is the time to do so."

There was an uncomfortable pause. Crew-members looked around, eyes searching for those willing to back out. A murmur passed over the crowd, but no one stepped forward.

"Are there any questions?" The chief paused. "The crew remaining behind will be in charge of the payload section, which will rendezvous with the departed main ship as soon as we complete our mission. If there are no questions, we should be on our way."

He turned and walked up the hydraulic ramp door followed by the officers and the volunteer crew. The command crew took its place on the bridge and commenced the departure sequence. In the cold blackness of space, the main ship fired its vertical lift-off thrusters and separated from the payload section. With a blinding flash of blue-green light from its engines, the ship vanished into the void of space.

The chief gave the order. "Go to maximum star drive, we must get to the Chelsea colony as soon as possible. Anjum, how long to Chaldean 5?"

Anjum checked his figures. "We should be coming out of star drive and into sub-star in about four and a half hours at our present speed. At that time we should be within orbiting distance of the planet."

****

GALACTIC COMMAND'S BATTLE cruiser Aurora was contacted by Commander & Chief Jones and instructed to rendezvous with the main OS One main ship at Chaldean 5. En route to the planet under siege, it encountered a strange looking nebula in its flight path. Captain Reese Rivera instructed his crew to scan the nebula and monitor its movements, color fluctuations and energy output.

"There is something very strange about this nebula. See if we can navigate around it," he directed his second in command. As the cruiser diverted its course around the nebula, Rivera noticed that the nebula was trailing at a distance and matching the cruisers speed and course.

"Sir, the nebula seems to be following us," the navigator observed.

"I don't like this," Captain Rivera said. "Go to alert status four and bring weapons hot."

"Sir, all weapons indicate green and ready," the weapons officer announced.

"Ensign, put that thing on ship-wide viewCOM." The captain went on voiceCOM and announced in an urgently, "This is not a drill, I repeat, this is not a drill. All hands to battle stations. Fire on my command." He turned to the pilot. "Go to maximum star drive. Lets see if we can outrun this thing."

As the ship shifted into maximum star drive, the nebula increased its speed beyond star drive maximum. Its color fluctuated from red to purple to blue and the shifts increased in frequency and intensity as it began closing in on the Aurora. "When that thing reaches a range of one thousand kilometers," Captain Rivera said to the weapons officer, "fire a burst of proton lasers directly into the heart of whatever that thing is."

Tension mounted as the creature closed in on the battle cruiser.

"Five thousand kilometers, four thousand kilometers, three thousand, two thousand, one thousand kilometers," the navigation officer announced.

"Fire proton laser canons," the captain ordered. The laser found its mark, disintegrating half of the creature in a ball of fire, but half of the creature remained and continued to pursue the cruiser.

"Fire again," the captain yelled.

Another burst from the proton lasers was on its way to its mark. The alien shifted its form causing the proton burst to miss its target. It sent out long tendrils that grabbed and wrapped around the ill-fated vessel, disrupting its energy flow. The ship began shaking violently throwing the crew off balance. Crewmembers reached and grabbed for anything to keep from falling. In desperation, the captain tried to contact engineering.

"See if you can stabilize the ship's power flow!"

The COMsystem, faded in and out from the energy fluctuation.

"Un...able...to stabile...explos...minent, I... expect three...minutes to structural collapse," came the reply.

Rivera slammed his fist down on the COMbutton. "Abandon ship!" he yelled to his crew. "Report to your assigned evacuation pod. Get the hell out of here. Our ship cannot withstand this attack much longer."

The crew started rushing to their assigned pods. As the frantic seconds went by, automatic computer-controlled bulkhead doors closed off corridors, stranding crewmembers all over the ship.

Internal explosions caused hull breaches and loss of pressurization. Crewmembers caught in the breaches were swept out into space to their deaths. Few were lucky enough to make their way through the smoke and scattered debris to their escape pods.

Outside the battle cruiser, the creature's energy intake was increasing exponentially by the second. Vital sections of the ship exploded as escape pods separated from the ship. Miraculously, Captain Rivera, in the command center, which doubled as its own escape vehicle, was able to activate the emergency thrusters and blast away from the doomed ship.

A final blast blew apart the rest of the ship. The resulting shockwave and flying hull debris destroyed the alien and any escape pods caught in its wake. Scattered chunks of debris hit the command escape vehicle causing it to tumble out of control. The hull of the pod was breached in several places and inside the captain and two officers lay on the deck badly injured.

Captain Rivera was crumpled, lying face down on the deck. There were several burns on his hands. His uniform was ripped and stained with blood from a wound on his back. The other two officers were lucky to be alive. One of them had a broken arm and the other could barely move his legs. Captain Rivera, hearing the moans of the injured men, slowly attempted to stand up. Feeling pain in every movement, he got up and turned to his officers. His vision was blurred from a concussion he received during the evacuation. From a small cut on his forehead, blood ran down his tanned face past his right eye. He limped toward the injured men, his vision clouded by the smoky haze. He reached down and, one by one, dragged his navigation officer and weapons specialist across the deck and strapped them in their chairs. The command module was tumbling through space, making it difficult to stand or walk. Reese took his place at the command console and strapped himself in. Most systems were not functional and those that remained were shorting out as the smell of burnt circuits filled the already smoky air.

The captain had no choice but to maintain the course and do what he could to keep life support systems functional. He had to make rendezvous with the OS One main ship. Fanning away some of the lingering smoke with his hand, he activated the altitude thrusters in short bursts to stop the craft from tumbling. He set a course for Chaldean 5 and prayed that the navigational systems were functional. Rivera managed a half smile as the craft turned in the programmed direction. Due to the external damage on the craft, star drive was out of the question; the only option was sub-star drive. He reached over to the toggle and slowly moved it forward.

The rear escape engines were hesitant to start, sizzling during the ignition process. Captain Rivera pulled the toggle back and pushed it forward a second time. The engines sputtered to life but only at half-thrust. He activated the emergency solar-sail system, which deployed itself outside the pod gathering nearby starlight and converting it into energy and thrust that would give them a fighting chance to reach Chaldean 5.

Captain Rivera tried to contact Galactic Command on viewCOM only to discover his long-range communications were out as well. He entered the code for the distress beacon on the recessed control panel in the arm of his command chair. The sudden sound of a proximity alarm shattered his thought pattern. He unbuckled himself from of the chair and limped over to the tactical viewCOM—another, but smaller, creature approached.

"In the first attack, the thing seemed to feed on our power output. If I shut down all power, perhaps it won't notice me."

As the creature approached the badly damaged command pod, it extended its deadly tentacles towards the craft. Rivera immediately shut down all power systems including thruster power. The tendrils, as if elastic stretched to its limit, retracted back into the nebula. The creature passed directly over the now-dead space pod, missing it by mere meters and continued on into deep space.

Captain Rivera did not want to take any chances by restarting systems too soon. He nervously waited with the knowledge that every precious minute lost could cost them their lives. After thirty-eight minutes, he entered the re-energizing sequence into the command computer and all workable systems came to life. The distress beacon resumed its normal sending pattern. He checked his drift rate and recalculated the course to Chaldean 5.

****

ON CHALDEAN 5, after four and a half hours of travel, OutStar One's main ship landed on the outskirts of the ravaged colony. The bright, sunny afternoon sky couldn't mask the death and destruction left behind by the cloud creatures. The crewmembers disembarked seeing clouds of smoke, small fires still burning out of control and ruins of what recently was a bustling city. It looked as if a squadron of enemy ships had bombed the place.

They walked slowly down the ramp and made their way cautiously toward the main gate of the city. Just on the other side, gruesome carnage was everywhere. The predator's giant sunken footprints stamped pits across the charred surface. Blackened, shriveled bodies of men and women littered the area and the stench of death hung in the breeze. The chief and his crew, weapons drawn, put on their toxin-filter masks as they pressed through the wreckage and destruction.

"Please don't touch anything," Dr Mutara shouted, loudly enough for all to hear. She looked down and scrutinized her scancorder. "I have a very faint life reading, six hundred meters north of our position, definitely human."

"If I remember the layout of this place correctly, that should be the communications tower," said Jack. The captain split the group into sections. "Seth and Jessica, lead your crews to search the colony for any signs of life, while the rest of you, come with me to the communications tower."

"Everybody look sharp," the chief said. "Those creatures could still be lurking around and could strike at anytime."

Commander Roberts noticed a blip on his scancorder and adjusted the frequency.

"Win, I think I located a distress signal about 75 meters northeast of our present position."

"Are you sure?"

"I know a distress signal when I hear one." Seth said, impatiently.

"OK, Seth, take Tapia and one member of the medical team in the hover jet. Be extremely careful and keep your emergency-tracking signal tuned to 7.5. Good luck." As the two officers and the medical assistant went back to the ship to procure a hover jet, the rest of the rescue party split up to search the colony for survivors.

****

THE COMMUNICATIONS TOWER was no more. A mountain of rubble seemed to grow out of the ground where it once stood. Captain Jones' scancorder beeped louder and louder as they honed in on what seemed to be the lone survivor of the massacre. The crewmembers dug through the piles of debris when they heard a faint, weak voice coming from the wreckage. Dr. Mutara gave explicit orders.

"Move through the rubble very carefully. Speed is not our primary aim. Whoever finds the victim is not to touch or move him or her. Call me immediately. Please proceed."

The crew continued their search, moving heavy chunks of metal and rock. Equipment from the communications center tangled with furniture and personal affects littered the sector. Captain Jones and Chief Mack jumped in to help.

"Over here, Doctor. I see something!" yelled Ensign Ryan, a young medical technician. Dr. Mutara carefully, but quickly, navigated her way over the rubble until she reached her protégé.

"Help…help. Please…" came a small voice from under a heavy sheet of titanium window casing.

"We are doing our best. Please hold on. We will have you free in a moment," called out Dr. Mutara. "Wingate, Jack, over here! We need help."

The commanding officers jumped over the piles of wreckage and aided the crew in removing the large metal slab from atop the injured man. His legs were crushed and useless, he bled from injuries to the head and abdomen, his face was a mess of tangled beard and blood.

"Dr. Mutara, how shall we proceed?" Jack asked.

"We will use that plank of metal," she said pointing to a long narrow section of door. "Bring it here and carefully lift him onto it, taking care not to move his spine. Sir," she continued, addressing the victim. "What is your name, sir?"

"My name is...Fin Ton...Jedidiah Fin Ton," he paused, gasping for air.

"It's okay Mr. Fin Ton. We are here to help you. Try not to speak." Dr. Mutara ran her scancorder over his body. She closed her eyes and took a deep breath. "Let's get him to the ship if possible."

Two med-techs carefully lifted Mr. Fin Ton onto the metal slab and carried him to what had been the public square. He whimpered in pain, but did not move. The doctor pulled aside Chief Mack and Captain Jones.

"Gentlemen, this man has extensive internal injuries. There is little I can do for him, even if he survives the trip back to the ship. I suggest we make him as comfortable as possible and see if he can give us any information that will be helpful in the investigation."

"Are you sure, Doctor? Shouldn't we try everything to save him?" Jack asked.

"Of course, Captain, and I will. But like I said, there is little I can do." Mutara walked alongside the makeshift gurney and offered Mr. Fin Ton some water from a container she carried in her shoulder case. "Easy...easy," she said. "Take small sips. We don't want you to choke." She smiled her warm smile at the dying man. He took comfort in her presence. Jack joined them.

"May I ask you a few questions, Mr. Fin Ton?" He looked at Dr. Mutara for approval and she nodded.

"Of...course...sir," Fin Ton replied.

"Was there any kind of warning before the attack began?"

"No, none...But I sensed something...before...." Fin Ton answered in a weak and desperate voice.

"What do you mean?" asked the chief.

"I got...an eerie...feeling." He stopped for a moment and shook his head apologetically. "I'm sorry...it's hard to...explain...but just before they hit, we...Lorell and I...felt...impact tremors... one, two, three...through the bottoms of our feet. The building shook...I thought it was...construction...at first...then we saw...these large, thick, black, smoke-like objects...moving towards us. We were... frozen...with fear as we watched...them split...into the same large objects...that surrounded...the outer...wall of the...colony." Mr. Fin Ton paused, coughing and gasping for breath. The med-techs carrying him stopped and set him down. Dr. Mutara took out her scancorder and did another reading. She looked at Wingate and Jack and shook her head. They all knew he didn't have much longer and they were still about two hundred meters from the ship.

"Mr. Fin Ton, I am going to give you a pain-removal scan. It won't fix your injuries, but it should take away most of the pain until we can get you to the ship's hospital."

"Thank you…Doctor." Mr. Fin Ton closed his eyes.

"Sir, may I ask you another question?" Chief Mack asked hesitantly.

"Of course, sir. I want…to help…you find this thing… this evil…"

"What happened after the colony was surrounded?"

"People in the…streets…were running and screaming, trying…to take cover. The creatures…had long…tentacles…that grabbed…at the people. But I did notice… something…Every time…it grabbed a child…the child disappeared. It would take…the children up…into its nuc…leus…and it would…just be…gone. Adults…were…burned and…left for dead. None of our…attempts to subdue…them seemed…to work…as a matter of fact…our proton-laser blasts only…seemed to make…them stronger."

"That's enough, Mr. Fin Ton. You don't need to go on. Save your strength." The chief pulled the captain aside. "Jack, this is exactly how the creatures we encountered behaved. But what has happened to the children? Were did they go? Corpses of the adults were left behind. Why not the children?"

"It's a mystery to me, Wingate."

Dr. Mutara received a COMlink signal.

"Doctor Mutara. Lt. Martinez. We have found no signs of life in the quadrant south of the ship."

"Keep searching," Doctor Mutara responded in a stern and determined voice. "There have to be others alive somewhere in this colony. I want every square inch of this colony searched, that means basements, subbasements, anyplace that someone could hide."

"Yes, doctor. Martinez out."

The doctor and her team continued to transport Mr. Fin Ton to the OutStar, and his condition continued to worsen. There was little hope for his recovery, but the doctor was determined. They were about ten meters from the ship when Fin Ton asked them to stop.

"Please, no...further. Let me go. There are...others to save...Don't waste time...on some...one...like me."

"Nonsense, Mr. Fin Ton. You are as important as anyone else and we are going to do all in our power to help you," Dr. Mutara reassured him.

"No...I've seen...them. There are...children. Save...them...Doctor...Leave me and...save them."

"Sir, there is no one else. Now, I will hear no more nonsense. Ensigns, continue on to the ship." The med-techs picked up Mr. Fin Ton and pressed on to the OutStar.

There...are...others...Save...the...children..." Mr. Fin Ton's voice trailed off.

A second signal came in over the doctor's COMlink.

"We have located some children in subbasement four of the school at the north end of the colony," reported Lt. Martinez.

"How bad is it?" the doctor asked.

"We have a couple of cases of shock, a few minor cuts and bruises and some broken bones, but as I'm sure you can imagine, they are incredibly shaken."

"How many are down there?"

"Nine, doctor, between the ages of six and fourteen."

"Try to keep them as calm as possible and we'll send a hover jet to transport them to the ship. We should get them out of there as soon as possible and get their injuries treated."

"Of course, Doctor. We will await the arrival of the hover jet. Martinez out."

"Good news, gentlemen, there are more survivors. Mr. Fin Ton, you were right. Mr. Fin Ton? Mr. Fin Ton?"

"He's not responding, Doctor," said Ensign McGregor. The med-tech administered CPR in attempts to revive the dying man. His attempts proved futile. "Dr. Mutara, he's gone."

Dr. Mutara knelt beside Fin Ton and held his hand for a moment. Captain Jones knelt beside her and put his hand on her shoulder. She looked at him and attempted a smile.

"You were right, Odette. There was nothing you could do," he reassured her. Jack stood and offered her his hand. She took it and he helped her to her feet. Awkwardly, Jack reached down to hug the tiny woman, and for the first time in their relationship, she allowed it. Chief Mack interrupted their brief embrace.

"Captain, what is Seth's status?"

The captain and Dr. Mutara stepped quickly apart, Jack's fair skin flushed pink with embarrassment. Odette brushed at her clothes and busied herself with the deceased Mr. Fin Ton.

"No word yet, Chief. Anjum, have you heard anything? "

"Nothing here," Anjum said.

"Contact him on your COMlink and find out what's going on. I don't want to lose anybody else on this mission." Chief Mack's face betrayed his worry.

"Yes sir," Lt. Sarwar replied. He pulled the COMlink from his transport case and entered the commander's code. "Lt. Sarwar to Commander Roberts, acknowledge."

At first the transmission was garbled but it cleared up.

"Yes, Lieutenant. Roberts here. How is everything going on your end?"

"We lost one survivor over here, but Martinez's unit found nine children in the northern part of the colony. Did you locate the source of the distress beacon?"

"Yes, we did. Captain Erious Rea Fielding, who works for Comet Impact Supply Company, crash-landed about five kilometers west of the colony. Her ship was destroyed and she lost her copilot, and it seems our cloud creatures are responsible."

"Tell Seth to wrap up his investigation and bring Captain Fielding back to the ship for an examination, and tell Tapia to report directly to me when they arrive." Chief Mack instructed Lt. Sarwar.

The chief and his officers returned to the ship and walked up the ramp to the command center. The med-techs took the body of Mr. Fin Ton to the hospital's morgue and two crewmembers prepared a hover jet to take Dr. Mutara to the school where the surviving children waited. Captain Jones and Chief Mack, followed by Lt. Sarwar, entered the command center through the hissing double doors. The captain noticed a red flashing indicator on the ship's communication console. He dashed over to it, motioning for the chief.

"It looks like we have a live one here!" He sat down pulled up the location-tracking screen. The chief walked over looking puzzled.

"What's going on?"

The captain wheeled around in his chair.

"We are receiving a signal from a distress beacon on the Galactic Command frequency."

"Can you boost his signal?"

"It's coming into range. I'll switch us over to audio." The captain hit the switch. There was intense static, and a voice that was barely detectable.

"This is…Rivera…of…destroyed…crew did not survive…we…need of assistance…do you copy…. OutStar."

"We were expecting a battle cruiser. This could be it. Can you do any better with his signal?"

The captain did his best to achieve a better connection between the main ship and the badly damaged Aurora command pod.

"Here we go, Chief. Captain Jack Jones of OutStar One. Please state your position."

"Captain, thank god. This is Captain Rivera of Galactic Command, Aurora. We were sent to assist you on Chaldean 5, but were attacked by an immense cloud-like creature. We are currently drifting about three kilometers above the planet's atmosphere, but given the distressed state of our ship and lack of operational power, we will not be able to attain the necessary speed for re-entry."

"We can't wait for Seth," Chief Mack informed Sarwar. "We have to go up and get them before they're caught in the planet's gravitational pull and burn up in the atmosphere. Inform the hover jet of our situation. Tell them that we are performing an emergency liftoff and that they are to report to the north quadrant to rescue the children in the school. Jack, tell Captain Rivera we are on our way."

"Yes, sir." Chief Mack called Dr. Mutara on the voiceCOM.

"Doctor, abort hover jet mission. We are sending Commander Roberts and Lt. Tunica. We have another rescue to make. Please prepare med-bay to receive injured members of Galactic Command."

"Sir," Lt. Sarwar reported, "we have a twenty-seven minute window to make contact with Aurora."

"Lieutenant, prepare for lift-off."

The engines started with a low whine that built to an intensely high pitch. The down blast kicked up dust below the ship's vertically positioned nozzles. The ship shook and vibrated as the chief pushed the throttle forward in small increments. Within seconds, the power buildup indicators flashed from red to standby amber to green and the vertical lift-off thruster engines ignited and lifted the craft, moving it straight up, slowly accelerating. OS One broke the first cloud cover and passed through the upper atmosphere, heading into space on an intercept course with the Aurora command pod. Captain Jones turned to the chief with a look of concern.

"We'll only get one chance at this, Wingate."

The chief shifted his gaze to the front viewscreen through which he could see the scarred and pitted craft heading in their direction. Lt. Sarwar appraised the situation.

"We have visual contact. We will be passing Aurora in four minutes, twenty-two seconds." Anjum worked feverishly to maintain a position parallel to that of the Aurora. "We have sixty seconds until contact." Captain Jones, from the tactical station, turned in his seat.

"Hey Anjum, you're cutting this awfully close."

"Contact in twenty seconds," the lieutenant angrily snapped, trying not to break his concentration. As the main ship approached the drifting pod, Sarwar maneuvered it into position to dock with the pod as the two crafts converged.

"Jack get a structural read out of the craft. We're going to have to bring her in manually with the arms," said the chief.

"Why can't we bring her in with our auto-magnetic system?"

"Anjum, just do what I say. I'll explain later. I'm going to the hatch to assist Captain Rivera and his crew once everything is secure."

"All right, Chief, whatever you say." Anjum maneuvered the OutStar closer to the Aurora. "OK Jack, do your stuff," he yelled.

A set of robotic arms extended from the outer wing of the main ship on each side of the hatch door. Knowing that one mistake could be fatal for all of them, he deftly manipulated the controls like a surgeon.

The arms reached out for the stock bar on the command pod. Without warning, two of the pod's side altitude thrusters fired unexpectedly, changing the pod's vector. Jack made a grab for the pod and missed. He watched it veer off and approach the fringes of the planet's atmosphere.

"Hey, did you see that?"

"Yes I did, and I know they didn't just fire their own thrusters. What the hell is going on over there? We lost it!" said an agitated Anjum.

"I know, I know, and if we don't get it soon, it is going be caught in the planet's pull," the Captain said. Tensions rose to fever pitch. "We have one more chance to do this thing right, otherwise, those men are dead." Lieutenant Sarwar changed course to catch up with the pod and maneuvered within docking distance for a second time.

"Anjum, move us a little bit closer to her," Jones instructed. "Ok, here we go again."

Sarwar moved the ship's airlock wing closer to the side of the command pod's airlock door, adjusting for pitch and angle with its own thrusters. Jack extended the arms and locked successfully on to the command pod's sidebars with a thud and pulled it into a secure docking position.

"All clear, we are locked on," Jones said with a sigh of relief.

The tension on board leaked away. Jones and Sarwar looked at each other with smiles of victory. Sarwar contacted Mack with the news.

"Good call, Chief. If we had used the magnetic beams, it would have pulled the pod in too quickly, and since the Aurora is in such bad shape, it might not have been able to handle the stress of the impact. We are in prime boarding position."

"Good work, Lieutenant." The chief shut off the COMsystem and wiped the sweat from his brow. He stepped in front of the docking control panel and activated the enclosure sleeve mechanism. It unfolded like an accordion, moving down on a track toward the inside airlock door of the wing and sealed itself around the door. On the other side of the door, a continuation of the same sleeve moved from out of its retainer housing and made contact with the airlock door sealing itself magnetically on the command pod airlock. The chief began the pressurization process and watched the barograph gauge climb from red to green in less than fifty seconds, achieving pressurization and artificial gravity. The green indicator light let the chief know that it was safe to open the main ship's airlock door.

Simultaneously, the doors of the two crafts slid open. The chief peered cautiously down the sleeve and saw smoke spilling out of the command pod into the sleeve chamber. Joined by Captain Jones and a team of medics, the chief entered the airlock and walked through the sleeve into the pod, where they heard moaning and coughing. They found Captain Rivera stumbling out of the pod carrying his flight recorder.

"There are two injured crewmembers in the forward compartment," Captain Rivera gasped. "There's also a ruptured pipe in there spewing Argon gas. We have to evacuate now. See that flashing red light on the panel? It means toxic fumes are building up."

With his eyes tearing from the smoke, the chief blinked repeatedly.

"Yes, I know, let's move!" Passing the first of the injured crewmembers to the med-techs behind them, the chief and Captain Jones rushed in to evacuate the rest of the pod's crew. Within minutes, all three members of Galactic Command's pod were safely aboard the OutStar One main ship and were being rushed to med bay. From his COMlink, Chief Mack contacted Sarwar in the command center.

"Jones and I are on our way back to the bridge. Prepare for disengagement."

****

ON THE CHIEF'S signal, Captain Jones activated the release sequence, closing the door to the main ship slowly and sealing the OutStar crew and passengers from the buildup of smoke and gas in the airlock. The crew watched on the viewscreen as the sleeve detracted and the friction caused sparks to flash from metal scraping against metal.

"Sarwar, I'm afraid that with the gas leak on the Aurora those sparks are going to ignite. Prepare the emergency thrusters and go on my command!"

"Yes, Chief. Ready."

"Jack, retract manual docking arms...Now! Thrusters...Now!"

As the OS One blasted away from the command pod, the Aurora was caught in the gravitational pull of the planet and exploded into flames as it picked up speed and blazed like a comet, sending flaming debris hurdling toward the surface of the planet below.

"Whew! That was a close one Chief!" Sarwar turned to Mack.

"Let's just get back to the others. I don't know if I can take anymore close calls."

7

Evidence

Lieutenant Martinez joined Chief Mack and Captain Jones in the command center. "We're glad you made it back safely. The children are aboard the ship and Dr. Mutara's team is attending them. She says you may interview them after they've had a chance to rest."

"I'm glad something went right. It was a close one up there. Let's get a head count and get back to the OutStar secondary. I, for one, need a drink."

"Yes, sir, so do I."

"Captain, Chief?" Lt. Tunica peeked her head through the command center door. "May I have a word?"

"Of course, Lieutenant, what's on your mind?" Mack replied.

"Sir, I have had a vision, which I think is important enough to investigate before we depart for the rest of OS One."

"What was it?" Jones asked, curiously.

"I saw a vague image of a human running from one of the alien predators. Then the image became sharper. A frightened man was being stalked by a being with a long tentacle. In the distance, he saw a door and made a dash for it. He pushed a button that opened the double doors, ran in and immediately pushed a button on the other side to close the doors. But the tentacle shot through, catching and entrapping the man. He screamed out in pain, his desperate cries echoed through the damaged corridor, but were unheard. The tentacle strangled the man before snapping off at the door."

The officers sat in silence as they listened to Tapia's account of her vision.

"Do you have any idea where this took place?" Lt. Martinez asked.

"It seems to be nearby. I sense a government building. I also sense that the being is trapped where it was injured. The vision became blurry, but I do not feel that it escaped."

"This may be our only chance of finding out what this creature is, Chief," Martinez said excitedly. "The communications center is just across the plaza from here—maybe that's where its stranded."

"Well, Jess, why don't you take Tapia and Seth and check it out," the chief reluctantly replied. "I would like to get us out of here sooner than later, but you're right. This may be our only chance to find out what is wreaking such havoc."

"Thanks, Chief. We'll try to make it quick."

****

COMMANDER ROBERTS AND Lieutenants Martinez and Tunica entered the badly damaged structure, stepping over the remains of an automatic door that lay twisted about bits of concrete. They were armed with proton pistols and brought with them an anti-gravity dolly and a special electro-magnetic containment chamber in which they hoped to capture the creature. In the faint glow of the surviving lights, they found two bodies buried under a section of wall. Rusty streaks of dried blood striped the floor. Tapia kneeled down to see if there was anything that could be done for them, but they were dead. The team continued to push inside and an alert signal chimed on the commander's scancorder.

"I'm getting an energy reading on a lower floor. But it could be one any one of several sub-basements."

"I'm getting the same reading here. It's definitely down below somewhere in this building. Can you pinpoint a location?" Tapia asked.

"No, but if we go to the bottom-most floor, we can work our way up until we find it," Martinez suggested.

Fortunately for the team, the power-lift at the end of the corridor was still operational. They entered and Seth pushed the button for sub-level four. The automatic doors closed and they descended into the bowels of the building. Tensions were high, and as the team moved deeper into the basement, the lift abruptly stopped at sub-level three.

"Why are we stopping here?" asked Martinez.

"Hell if I know," said the commander. "But with the hit this place took, I'm surprised this thing is working at all. Let's take the stairs."

The doors opened into an area partially illuminated by lights that flickered like strobes over the wrecked corridor. The team turned right out of the lift and moved cautiously down the corridor. The strange energy reading was getting stronger as they turned the corner. At the end of the passageway, they came to two closed doors.

The commander moved his scancorder in slow sweeping motions across the doors. He stopped and turned to his crew.

"Whatever we are looking for is behind these doors." Silently, the team drew their proton pistols from their holsters.

"I don't think these doors are going to open," said Tunica.

"You're probably right. Usually you have to have an access code," said Martinez.

"Let's try the lighted switch on the panel, anyway," Seth interjected.

"No time. Get back and take cover," said Martinez. With two blasts of her pistol, the heavy doors fell from their tracks and hit the floor with a resounding thud.

"Well, forget the access code," Roberts smirked.

The team waded through the debris and through the doorway.

"Look!" Seth pointed out a small dark smoke-like object about a meter in diameter. Its shape kept changing but it did not dissipate. Bits of pulsating blue-green light emanated from its core and five long silvery tendrils were flailing about, one was caught in another door. "Do you see that?"

"Seth, that is what attacked us on UC-788, only this one is much smaller," Martinez said.

"It's caught and seems to be weakened. It's just like in my vision—the man I saw will be on the other side of that door," Tapia explained.

"Well, let's try to get it," the commander instructed.

A nervous Martinez carefully maneuvered the containment chamber toward the smoke entity. She stopped about a meter and a half from her quarry. Edgy and nervous, Seth and Tapia watched with weapons poised. Martinez activated the containment chamber from the control panel on the rear of the unit. A small door opened at the front of the chamber. Martinez turned a dial that created a magnetic field inside the chamber. The field strengthened and emitted a high-pitched hum.

Suddenly, the alien creature moved toward the chamber, pulling at the tentacle caught in the door. Its bright color core changed and fluctuated inside the dark smoke. It's tendrils spread in all directions as it reached for the opening of the chamber.

Seth carefully drew his proton pistol and fired at the trapped tentacle. The blast snapped the tendril and the creature flew across the room into the containment crate. Martinez closed the containment door and trapped the creature.

A sigh of relief escaped from the crew.

"Good work, Jess." Seth congratulated her.

"I didn't do anything. You released it from its hold."

"That's what I call teamwork," quipped Tapia.

"Okay, let's get this thing out of here, but go easy. We don't want anything to go wrong now." Seth worriedly followed behind his friends as they took the corridor that led to the power lift.

****

"READY. ALL STATIONS read full power for vertical thruster lift-off. Ignite all engines," the captain announced. The engines engaged with a roar and began to lift the heavy weight of the ship, moving it straight up on a vertical vector.

"As soon as we clear the planet's atmosphere, set a course for OutStar secondary and go to Star drive 9.9. I want to get back as soon as possible. I'll feel better when that thing is in a more secure place," Chief Mack ordered.

Sarwar activated star drive, pushing the craft forward at an incredible speed, leaving behind Chaldean 5 and all that happened there.

Less than hour into the flight, a transmission came over the viewCOM. Leo J. Chance appeared on screen.

"We tried to contact you at the colony but got no response. Were you able to find anything?"

"More than you can imagine, sir," Captain Jones reported. "In fact…"

"Excuse me…" Chance cut off Jack. "It seems we lost contact with the battle cruiser Aurora commanded by Captain Rivera that was to rendezvous with you on Chaldean 5. We are still trying to find out what has happened. We were hoping they have merely had a technical glitch with their COMsystem. Did it ever reach you?"

"Well Captain Chance," said the chief. "The situation is not good, not good at all. What we saw on the viewCOM when the attack was taking place was bad enough, but what we found was totally incomprehensible. As for your battle cruiser…it was destroyed."

"How could that happen? That ship carries enough fire power to sweep through an asteroid field."

"Look, Chance, you don't seem to understand what we are dealing with," Jack countered. "There is a destroyed colony on Chaldean 5 with over forty-one hundred dead. They were swept up like candy by these things. By some miracle, the Aurora's command module survived an attack by the same aliens that destroyed this colony."

"How do you know that's what actually happened?" asked Chance, clenching his teeth.

"We have three surviving crew members from the command pod, Captain Rivera and two of his officers. They are now recuperating under the care of Dr. Mutara and her medical staff."

Chance lowered his head, and then raised it, the rage in his voice turned into a soft whisper of concern. "Are they OK? Will they survive?"

"Yes. According to the doctor, there were some broken bones, internal bleeding and head injuries, but they should be fine in time."

"Good."

"Well, we have another surprise for you." The chief's words made Chance straighten up in his seat.

"What surprise?"

"We managed to capture and contain part of the smoke-creature."

Chance's eyes widened with surprise and he became eerily calm. "You mean to tell me you actually captured part of the monster?"

"Yes, we have, and we are en route to OS One secondary to analyze it."

"This is a very serious situation and I am ordering you to report with the alien to the Earth base of Galactic Command Intelligence, as soon as possible. Galactic Command can take over the investigation from here. We also want to debrief everyone involved in the Chaldean 5 incident. This debriefing will be kept classified in order to avoid a system-wide panic." He paused for a moment, rubbing his neck while moving his head from side to side as if trying to relieve some of the building tension.

"Wait a minute. We have risked our necks to help you and you want to just cut us out?" Martinez interjected. "Seth and I caught the creature ourselves, after we were attacked by one just like it. I should have a chance to do my own research on it. We have just as much invested in this as you do."

"I'm sorry, but we have to think of what is good for the galaxy. I'm sorry if your scientific pride is hurt, Lieutenant, but there is no debate on this issue. Chief Mack, report to GC immediately or I'm afraid we won't be able to compensate you for your mission."

"What? That's outrageous!" The chief jumped to his feet. "Listen, Chance. Don't threaten me. We have risked life and limb for you and Galactic Command, so unless you want me to go over your head to TESSA, you will pay us what we are due. And you could at least let my scientists have a crack at the mystery."

"We will discuss this further when you arrive. Chance out."

8

Intelligent Life

CHIEF MACK, CAPTAIN JONES AND Lt. Martinez walked silently to the medical bay. They had a lot of work to do before OutStar One reached space station Serenity. Martinez was still seething from her run-in with Chance.

"I don't trust that man. He has been hostile and uncooperative since we started this mission. And we're doing him a favor. No offense, Jack, your father seems very fair and reasonable, but these Galactic Command guys have a lot to learn about dealing with people."

"It's okay, Jess. Why do you think Win and I left? Chance has always been kind of a renegade. I had a run in with him when I was a cadet and he never let me forget it. I think it bothered him that I was the C & C's son and he challenged me at every turn."

"I don't trust him either. Obviously we are not doing this for the money, but to threaten us like that. Something is definitely fishy there."

The officers entered the medical bay. Dr. Mutara greeted them warmly.

"Lt. Martinez, I am so glad you are here. We should get started right away on the analysis of the creature."

"Yes, ma'am. I'm ready. Win, Jack, I'll see you later." Lieutenant Martinez proceeded on to prepare for her examination.

"Gentlemen, how can I help you?"

"We would like to speak with some of your patients. Rivera and Fielding must have some vital information we could use," Jones explained.

"And, if you think they are up to it," Mack tentatively inquired, "I would like to speak to some of the children, as well."

"Well, the grown-ups are all yours, but I don't think the children are ready to relive the horrors of the past couple of days. I will let you know when you can speak with them."

"Of course, Doctor."

"Follow me, and I will take you to Captains Rivera and Fielding."

****

"Well, the only thing I can add is, I think these creatures are intelligent. How far in advance of ours is the big question," Rivera said.

Why do you think they have intelligence?" Captain Jones asked.

"If something follows you and change course as you do, it must have some sort of intelligence. They are also capable of traveling at great speeds, exceeding our own star drive maximum," Rivera continued. "What we don't know is the limit of their communications and how many of them are out there."

"Whatever the hell they are, they move fast. I had no time to do anything but eject my emergency life pod to save my own life." Captain Fielding joined the conversation.

Captain Rivera reached over and put a friendly hand on Fielding's shoulder to comfort her. Fielding put her own hand on his in kind and smiled at the gesture.

"Thank you, both for your input. I won't trouble you anymore. You should rest," the chief said. "If you can remember anything else, please let us know."

****

"Jack, this is the Chief," he said over the COMlink. We will be coming up on space station Serenity orbiting Earth in about five hours at our present speed. I think it's a good time for you to eat and get some sleep. The rescue team should do the same."

"Ok, Wingate. Let me know when to take over. I'll be in one of the rest quarters on deck two. COM out."

Dr. Mutara walked up behind the Captain, startling him.

"Oh! Doctor. I didn't see you there."

"I'm small and stealth," she joked, looking squarely at him. "Captain, I just noticed something, let me take a look at you." She put her hand on his forehead to see if he had a fever. Her touch was cool on his blazing forehead. "You are burning up and you look pale," she said, noticing a slight discoloration on his face. "Do you have a headache?"

"Headache? Yes I do."

"Let me give you something for it."

"No thank you, doctor," said the captain. "You know how I feel about taking medicine, besides it's not that bad. All I need is some food and a little rest."

Doctor Mutara put her hand on his arm. "Well if you change your mind, you know where to find me." The captain nodded in agreement and squeezed the doctor's hand.

****

As the OutStar main ship sped its way through space toward Earth, two and a half days of travel at star drive 8.6 had finally put them in proximity to Earth's solar system. Communication with the back-up crew of the OutStar payload section had been established while in transit to update them on all that happened. The main ship, moving past planets and moons, approached space station Serenity, orbiting kilometers above Earth. Serenity was a technological gem. There was a seemingly endless stream of ships taking on and discharging cargoes and people. It was the gateway from Earth to the stars.

An exhausted Jack entered the command center of the main ship, walked over and took his seat next to Wingate. The chief glanced at the captain.

"Man, I feel the way you look. By the way, you never told me how it went with the questioning."

"Ahh...it went well."

"Shutting down sub-star drive, going to thruster power, preparing for atmospheric approach," Anjum interrupted

Tapia heard an intermittent signal and noticed the small green flashing light just below the viewCOM screen. "Hey Chief, we have an incoming viewCOM transmission. An image of Commander & Chief Jones appeared.

Before the he could speak Seth asked, "Are you preparing a security team for our arrival with the creature?"

"We have a small contingent awaiting your arrival. Don't worry. You will be accompanied. Inform your pilot to land in landing bay platform eleven, Galactic Command out." The screen went blank and ended with a tone.

"Bye, Dad," joked Jack. "Man that was short and straight to the point."

The chief reached over and pushed the button on the internal COMsystem informing all on board to stow loose equipment, strap in and prepare for a gravity change prior to docking.

"What a sight," said Captain Jack. Even after experiencing more reentries than he could count, he still couldn't shake the feeling he got when returning to the mother planet. "It's always good to be home, even under the present circumstances," he said, viewing Earth on the large, front viewscreen.

The ship suddenly took a dive that caught the crew off guard. As the ship began to pick up unwanted speed, the first layers of thin atmosphere slipped past the ship's surface causing a heat build up. The computer announced the climb in hull temperature, warning lights flashed and loud alarms sounded continuously. The ship began to vibrate, shaking the crew in their seats as the calm and serenely artificial computer voice echoed within the command center.

"Re-entry shields heating, hull temperature three hundred-ten degrees and climbing, three hundred-fifty degrees." Pulse rates began to climb as well. Everyone watched Anjum closely as the hull temperature reached four hundred degrees.

"OK, Anjum, I think you better start to slow us down before I take over the controls," quipped Captain Jones.

"Don't worry guys, I know what I'm doing," Sarwar said confidently, smiling as he maneuvered the flight controls, changing the ships vector from a vertical nose dive to a horizontal glide path slowing the ship's decent. Sarwar held his concentration. He applied more power to the vertical thrusters causing the ship to slow down and counteract the earth's continuous gravitational pull. The computer voice announced the results of his actions.

"Hull temperature dropping within tolerance levels." The warning lights stopped flashing and the intermittent alarms were silenced. Sarwar put the ship back on an even keel, making its drop status satisfactory. Silently, the chief turned to Anjum, with a look that could kill.

"Chief, before you bite my head off, think about this, when was the last time we tested the main ship's flight warning systems under these kind of conditions?"

"What?" The chief was surprised and annoyed at the actions of his lieutenant commander. "You mean to tell me, you picked now to do a flight warning test?" The voice of an angry Dr. Mutara came on the voiceCOM.

"Who's minding the store in the command center? Have you forgotten? We have injured men, women and children on board this ship."

"I'm sorry, Doctor. It won't happen again." The chief's eyes focused back on Sarwar. "Command Center out."

"Prepare for slightly more than a bumpy ride from here on in, we are going to hit some heavy cross winds." The atmospheric indicators lived up to their prediction. The OutStar began to catch more turbulence as it descended, vibrating and tossing the ship, forcing Lt. Sarwar to compensate constantly.

The main ship continued in its descent, breaking through the afternoon cloud cover. It transitioned from a near vertical drop to a smooth forward motion as it came in over the Atlantic Ocean heading toward New York City. Galactic Command sent four military sky runners to meet them, clear a path through the air traffic and escort the main ship to its final destination.

"Boy! They are not fooling around!" A surprised chief was monitoring them on the viewCOM screen.

A communications link was established with the OutStar main ship by one of the sky runner's flight personnel and they were instructed to follow.

The ship glided over the Empire State Building heading downtown toward Wall Street, the sky runners, one on each side of the ship and one in the rear, broke formation to move forward and join the lead car as they continued to clear a path through a heavily populated air lanes of private and commercial aerial activity, and soared over the East river directly to Galactic Command Headquarters in the old Brooklyn Navy yards for a smooth rooftop landing.

Their escort job completed, the four sky runners blasted away like shooting stars onto another assignment. A signal came over the viewCOM and was acknowledged by Win, who activated the screen. The harried face of a man in Galactic Command uniform appeared.

"OutStar One, this is tower officer Ling. I have you on my screen and your approach is good. At this time you should be able to see the landing pattern lit, denoting bay eleven."

"Yes, we have visual, tower," said the chief, "and are we glad to be home, even if only for a short while."

"Yes, I can imagine how you feel. The rumor mill has been working overtime. Things are really buzzing."

"Well, I can tell you one thing, we won't disappoint you." Jack was cracking a slight smile.

Anjum moved the ship forward, hovered into position for a few seconds and achieved a soft touchdown on the tarmac directly over the recessed target landing lights.

Once settled, the ship's pressure valves on the bottom of the hull began releasing geyser-like vapors at three-second intervals. The Galactic Command troops lined up in rows of three on either side of the airlock, creating a center isle from the ship one hundred meters to the automatic entrance doors of Galactic Command.

"This is a small contingent?" asked Jack, getting up from his chair. "I see they are not taking any chances with our cargo." He reached over to turn on the internal COMsystem.

"Doctor Mutara and the rescue team, please assemble at the main airlock ramp door for departure."

****

THE CREW WALKED down the ramp, overwhelmed by the reception they received. The fresh smell of Earth filled the lungs of the rescue team, replacing the stale recirculated air of the ship and the burning smell of death they had become so familiar with. A stout, boxy man wearing the standard blue Galactic Command pants and jacket approached the chief.

"You must be Chief Operations Officer Mack. The Commander & Chief will be meeting with you shortly." His voice sounded throaty but strong, as he reached out to shake the chief's hand.

"Yes I am," said the chief as their hands met in a tight grip and released.

"Please, you all may follow me."

The crew disembarked, along with the group of rescued children. Parents had been notified and were waiting to retrieve them. Bringing up the rear of the OS One delegation, Captain Jones led the anti-gravity dolly carrying the magnetic containment chamber and the cloud-creature. Maneuvering the unit was Lt. Commander Sarwar with Lt. Martinez to his left. They moved in slow but steady steps, guiding the unit down the ramp.

Gasps rippled through the crowd when they saw the special cargo. Anjum continued to move out from under the ship into the light, which seemed to get dimmer, as if a dark cluster of clouds was forcing its way in to get a closer look. There was a sudden drop in the light level that threw a scare into the onlookers. The security team walked alongside the unit with drawn weapons set to kill mode and nervous trigger-fingers at the ready. The crowd on either side of the isle was paralyzed with fear, watching the alien form inside the containment chamber change shape as the unit moved by. The noise from the creature was a low rumble. A security officer met the crew half-way and told the chief to accompany her to the security wing of Galactic Command where the creature would be quarantined and given to the research team.

They passed through the huge doors, which were kept open. Not much had changed since Chief Mack and Captain Jones had been a part of Galactic Command. Newly designed column-lighted panels stood out from the beige-colored walls and the catwalk-like floor design, but, otherwise, Galactic Command's architecture had remained the same.

Captain Chance, Commander & Chief Jones and two research team members, with their white lab coats flapping in the breeze, approached from the opposite direction at a brisk pace. The two scientists hovered around the containment chamber with curiosity and excitement.

"O.K. I'll take over from here," Chance said in an authoritative manner. Anjum looked over at Mack who nodded his head. A twisted smile came over Chance's face as he looked at the crew of OutStar One. "Thank you ladies and gentlemen, you've all done a fine job. You are no longer needed and are free to depart at any time."

"Like hell we will," yelled the chief, his blood pressure and anger rising. "We are not going quietly. Whether you like it or not we are involved and we will stay. We took one hell of a risk to bring that damned thing here and we intend to find out just what we're up against."

Commander & Chief Vincent Jones interrupted, pointing his finger at Win.

"Chief Mack, you are out of line and out of your jurisdiction. You and your crew are to leave this matter to Galactic Command. Is that understood?"

Before the chief could answer, an angry Captain Jones exploded.

"Wait a minute, just because you're my father, don't think I won't say anything." He pointed his finger at the C & C. "You're the one that's out of line. Remember, you asked us for help," he paused for a moment, and then continued. "Wait a minute, let me rephrase that. You begged us to go on this mission, knowing how dangerous it would be and now you want to cast us aside like a used tissue!"

The Commander & Chief was embarrassed at being dressed down by his son in such a manner, but knew he had no defense against the truth. He looked at his angry son, thinking to himself how to defuse the situation before it got out of hand? Trying to calm things down a bit, he spoke in a non-confrontational voice.

"You're right, I did ask you to go and I also share your concern, but do understand that it is my intent to keep you posted as to anything our researchers discover. Realize that we are well equipped for research and analysis. I admit Chance and I came off a little rough and I apologize." Chance frowned in anger, but kept silent.

"I appreciate everything that you have done. As you already know, this matter is to be discussed with no one. There will be a board of inquiry on the Chaldean 5 incidents as soon as the medical needs of those involved are taken care of."

"Wait a minute! You mean to tell me that we are not included in the debriefing? Then why are we here? Why didn't you just send someone to pick up the thing if that's all you wanted?" Chief Mack demanded.

"Safety is of supreme importance and we felt this was the best way to transport the creature," a stern-faced C&C replied, standing his ground.

9

Friend Or Foe

TWO DAYS ELAPSED AFTER THE departure of the crew of OutStar One and Chance was placed in charge of the investigative research team with the task of examining the newfound entity.

In the laboratory, Chance was assisted in his investigation by a non-human Stealth named Code. A repetitive but quiet beep broke the silence.

"Sir, I think that was an incoming distress call."

"Good observation on your part." Chance glared at him. "However, you're being paid to take orders, not to think. What you thought was a distress call was a glitch that I have been trying to work out for days. Get me a frequency oscillator from the utility compartment since you're so eager to help."

Code left the room and shut the door behind him. Chance went to the viewscreen. He turned on the translator and there, appearing before him, was a cloud-creature.

"You almost got us caught. I have told you to use my personal secured channel which is linked to my quarters," Chance scolded.

The cloud-creature vibrated and pulsed. A computerized voice came through the COMsystem. "When you start living up to your agreements, I'll be more careful with your safety."

"Look, the OutStar crew has been dispatched and should be out of our hair, so to speak. They are only in business to make money. They've played the hero and now they are out of the picture."

"Their scientists have found one of the escaped soldiers and they have examined 2LM35 extensively. If you are not more careful, they are going to uncover the entire enterprise."

"If I'm not more careful? Your nanocons are the ones who got caught. All I did was get 2LM35 out of the OutStar's clutches. You're lucky I am as well connected as I am. If anyone other than me was heading this investigation, it would be all over the galaxy by now. You would be exposed and Galactic Command would have no choice but to attack."

"Enough of your impertinence. You may hold a secure position in Galactic Command, but you are disposable to us. We need about thirty more of the human children to complete our experiments."

"Look, I gave you an entire colony. One more attack and this thing will blow wide open. It's hard enough covering this thing up as it is."

"And you've been paid very well for your efforts. That can always stop, though. If you don't want to participate anymore, Chance, you are free to walk away."

"I'm sure you'd let that happen."

"Well, we would hate to see such a loyal servant to the residents of the galaxy be stripped of all honor, position and wealth. How would the people you serve, as Captain of Galactic Command, react if they knew you were selling their children for genetic experiments? If you don't deliver, Chance, you will be exposed."

"Fine. There is one more place—The Ecliptic World. It's a utopian outpost in the Canas Major Galaxy. Most of the residents are families with children and they do an extensive tourist business. I think you will find what you need there."

"Good. See how easy that was, Captain? Make the arrangements and I'll supply the nanocon power. And let's see if we can keep the OutStar crew out of it this time."

"Consider it done. Chance out."

Code returned with the frequency oscillator. Captain Chance took it from him and continued the pretense of research on the captured creature, 2LM35.

****

"WE ARE ON final approach and OS One secondary has cleared us for docking," Lt. Sarwar announced to the command crew. The main ship maneuvered into position and lowered itself on to the payload section of the craft. The landing went smoothly and the belly ramp door extended into the payload section airlock door. An accordion-like sleeve rose up from its recessed position and attached itself to the hull of the main ship making an airtight seal. A computerized voice came over the internal COMsystem.

"Pressurization is achieved."

The chief went to the voiceCOM and made an announcement to the crew.

"We have been through a lot in the past few days, I don't know how this is going to end, but we do need to unwind and get back to some sense of normalcy, whatever that's suppose to be. Please take this afternoon for rest and relaxation. Mack out."

The command deck crew smiled and nodded their heads in agreement as the chief continued.

"As for us, we are having a press conference at 16:00."

"What? We don't get to play?" Seth asked.

"Nope. If Galactic Command doesn't want us to be a part of their investigation, then I see no reason to keep this information to ourselves. The people represented by TESSA have a right to know that their lives and their children's lives are in danger. Go take showers, get cleaned up and meet me in the conference arena at 14:30."

****

THE RESCUE TEAM that visited Chaldean 5 was assembled on a dais facing four rows of half-circular tables, each supporting five viewCOMs. One by one, reporters logged in to the conference and their visages appeared on the screens. Chief Mack stood and walked to the glass podium.

"Ladies and gentlemen of the universal press, welcome to OutStar One. As you know, the galaxies of Alteria and Venga have been under attack by mysterious cloud creatures that kill and maim at random and leave few survivors. Galactic Command has tried to keep this information from the public. But we at OutStar feel that the public has a right to protect themselves and their families and, therefore, a right to know of these dangers.

"You were all given our official statement, so I will open the floor to questions. Yes, row 1, COMthree."

"Silvia Ray of Nova News. Galactic Command has given no indication that the events on Alteria UC-788 or Venga Chaldean 5 pose a threat to the general public. Can you describe the kind of threat you believe exists?"

"Yes, my crew has been personally attacked twice by the cloud-creatures Galactic Command is hiding from you. We lost six scientists on UC-788. They were burned alive by the monster. On Chaldean 5, forty-one hundred people lost their lives and four hundred children disappeared without a trace. We now believe, after extensive research by our own scientists, that the creatures are kidnapping the children and laying waste to anyone or anything else in their way. Yes, row three, COMfive."

"Tanka Ng of YTMO News. What exactly are the creatures? What do they look like?"

"Perhaps, Lieutenant Jessica Martinez can answer that." Jessica rose and walked to the podium as Wingate took his seat.

"Thank you, Chief. If you will turn your attention to the screen behind me, you will see pictures of the monsters." An audible gasp was heard from the COMs. "We have discovered that though the creatures look like clouds of smoke, they are actually made up of trillions of microscopic nano-robots. We were able to retrieve several of them from tissue samples taken from deceased victims and from examining one of the captured creatures ourselves. They posses an intelligence comparable, if not superior to our own. The nucleus of the creature is a ball of gaseous toxin that is highly flammable and resistant to most firepower. The only way we have found to destroy the creature is to overload the nucleus with great blasts of proton laser. Each creature, no matter the size, possesses six tentacles that carry an electric charge and can subdue the strongest of beings. They are used for walking, grabbing and defense. Are there any more questions? Yes, row two, COMtwo."

"Hellman Parker, Phoenix Press. Why is Galactic Command keeping this a secret?"

"I'll take this one, Lieutenant." Captain Jack Jones rose and took the podium. "It is our belief that there is corruption within Galactic Command that goes very close to the top. We do not know the extent of involvement, but we do suspect that the cover-up protects high-ranking officials. I encourage all of you to do a little digging of your own. Perhaps together we can bring a corrupt Galactic Command to justice."

Chief Mack joined Captain Jones at the podium.

"Thank you for your attendance. That is all we have time for today. We will keep you abreast of any new developments and hope that you will do likewise. Thank you. COMs out."

****

Two and a half weeks had passed since the press conference, and everything was going as smooth as could be expected under the circumstances. No more attacks were reported and the backlash the OutStar crew expected from their breech of Galactic Command security never came. Chief Mack, Captain Jones and Commander Roberts were discussing Captain Chance in the rec lounge over drinks.

"The bits and pieces of data on Chance we compiled definitely points to the fact that he is up to something, and it isn't good," Seth said. "But it seems that we are all in agreement that more evidence is needed to convince the counsel at Galactic Command."

Win and Jack nodded their heads. After taking a swig of grantar tea to clear his throat, Jack weighed in.

"You're right, we must have more substantiated proof. I hate to imagine the consequences that would ensue if we made any more accusations concerning the second in command. All we can do is wait and see what his next move will be." Wingate and Seth nodded approval.

The viewCOM across the room received a transmission and Seth got up to open the channel. He recognized a face that put a smile on his own.

"Captain Fielding! I can't believe it's you."

Captain Erious Rea Fielding greeted him with a smile in her new Comet Impact Supply Company uniform.

"What's new on the OutStar?" she asked enthusiastically.

"So far, everything has been quiet," Seth answered. "What can I do for you?" She looked at him and grinned.

"Look behind me." She indicated the ship commissioned to her. Seth could not believe his eyes. Her ship resembled something out of a men's locker room—peeling paint, dull lighting and seating that looked like it was bought at a junkyard. He shook his head in disgust.

"The company gave me this heap temporarily until I'm assigned one of the newer cargo ships. It's all I can do with my crew of seven to keep this bucket of bolts from falling apart. My hydrazine reactor coolant system failed, so it had to be taken off line. I am currently deploying my thrusters, shutting them down periodically to keep from exhausting my fuel supply. I'll need them for docking. In other words, I need your help and the company is willing to pay you to make the repairs, if that's all right with you."

"No problem. What's your ETA?"

"About four hours, I also have a lot to share with you....information that is..."

"I can't wait to see you in person." Seth smiled as his tanned cheeks turned pink. "See you when you arrive, viewCOM out."

Wingate and Jack watched with amusement.

"So Rea is coming to see you, huh?" Jack teased. "I hope you can keep your foot out of your mouth while she's here."

"Funny, coming from the guy who turns into a puddle every time Dr. Mutara looks in his direction," Seth retorted.

"I do not," Jack lied, taking his turn at blushing. "We are colleagues…nothing more." He got up and fixed himself another cup of tea.

"You know, it's been a while since we heard from Rea. I wonder what kind of debriefing she got from Galactic Command?" Win wondered aloud.

"Knowing those bastards, they probably told her she was mistaken and that nothing really happened, but then gave her a good threat just to be on the safe side."

"Mr. Roberts, I know you will want to handle the arrival particulars and make the necessary preparations for the damage-assessment party to board her ship."

"I'm on it," said Seth with the smile and left the rec lounge to make preparations for her arrival.

****

"COMMANDER ROBERTS, THERE has been a break-in in the computer records room on deck two, section seven," Security Officer Fisher reported.

"I'm on my way. Roberts out." Seth contacted Tapia via COMlink as he ran to his quarters to pick up his proton blaster. "Tapia, can you get down here to handle the arrival of Captain Fielding? I have something to attend to, Seth out." He reached deck two, section seven and met up with his security crew who were already on the scene.

Seth, on point, and his security force cautiously entered the computer room with weapons drawn. The room was dark with only the dim light from the computer screens and illuminated function buttons providing light. They sensed a presence as their eyes began to adjust to the near darkness.

Suddenly, blasts from a type-three proton pistol missed them by inches, striking the door and the opposite wall. The flash of heat forced them back outside to take cover. They returned fire to the vicinity where the blasts originated. The firefight heated up, with the blasts hitting and destroying computer screens and control panels.

"Damn!" Ensign Hoff yelled as she fell to the ground, wounded by a shot from the intruder's pistol. The crewmembers choked and coughed trying to breath through the stench of burning dura-plastic and rubber.

Seth, in a surprise move, lunged forward while firing his proton pistol, leapt over the console, knocked over and pinned down the intruder using his knees to hold down the violator's elbows.

"I've got him. Get over here."

Ensign Fisher turned on the light, illuminating the smoke filled room. Two crewmembers grabbed fire extinguishers and put out the fires. Turner and Mug took custody of the prisoner as the commander got up from the floor.

"Take him to a secure cell while I inform the chief." He looked around at the damage as the smoke dissipated. "Oh man, what a mess!" he said, following his security team to the holding cell.

****

THE COMMAND TEAM arrived on the cellblock. Annoyed and angry, Chief Mack walked over to the wall COMsystem and contacted the technical team in the computer room.

"What's the damage to the records room? Can any data be retrieved?"

"We have a damage control team working on the situation, sir. We should know something in a couple of hours."

Anjum walked over to the cell and asked the prisoner why he was here.

"Because it was easy."

Seth rolled his eyes at the suspect.

"What is your name? How did you break through the security on OS One and obtain access to our security lock-outs?"

To their amazement, the prisoner replied with arrogant confidence. "I have been here before extracting medical records. You figure it out."

"Let me tell you something," Wingate threatened. "You're in big trouble, so you can either answer our questions or we turn you over to Galactic Command."

"Who do you think sent me?" he smugly replied.

"What did you say?" Jack froze in his tracks. He took a deep breath, walked up to the cell and pressed the entry button. The bars slid open and he entered the cell. To everybody's surprise, he grabbed the prisoner by the collar and slammed him against the cell wall.

"You better give us some real answers now or you won't be able to give any after I get finished with you."

"You can't do this to me. I have my rights," the Stealth yelled out.

"Yes, you do, but we are neither military nor political. We do not go by their rules. Besides, no one knows you're here. We can do what we want with you. So you better come up with some answers and quick."

The strange prisoner thought for a moment and nodded his head, agreeing. Jack slowly released his grip cautiously and moved back a few steps giving the detainee some breathing room. He took a moment to catch his breath, and began.

"I am a Stealth. Maybe you have heard of us." Seth joined the conversation.

"As far as I know, TESSA has been trying unsuccessfully for a long time to get your government to join the alliance, but your people's isolationist policies forbid it. That still doesn't explain why you broke into the OS One med-lab or how you managed to get away undetected."

The Stealth was suddenly afraid. He only worked for Chance to help his people. If it were to come out on his home planet that he mixed with other races, he would be shunned.

"My name is Code. I have been secretly working for Captain Chance for six months. One of my abilities, unknown to most, is the ability to change my habiliments. It makes me very valuable in covert situations."

"What do you mean you can change your habiliments?" Seth asked.

The Stealth, realizing he would have to demonstrate, prepared to shift shape. Jack, not knowing what to expect, cautiously backed away and put a nervous hand on his proton pistol. The rest of the crew outside the cell followed his lead. With his eyes closed, the Stealth extended his arms outward, and then raised them upward as if praying. Time seemed to slow down as the Stealth changed the molecular structure of the clothing he was wearing to make it look like an OS One uniform.

Looking on in astonishment, the crew couldn't believe their eyes. Then the Stealth changed from the OS One uniform back to his original manner of dress, a long white caftan-like shift.

"I also have the ability to link up to any computer system by mere touch and can access and download data into my memory."

"So you were gathering information on everything that has taken place, the attack on the colony, the dead child and everything in between," said Captain Jones, releasing the grip on his proton pistol. The Stealth nodded his head in agreement.

"And you've been collecting this data for Chance?"

"Yes, Captain, you're correct," replied Code.

"I knew it! Wingate this is just the evidence we need to expose Chance."

"Assuming he'll cooperate."

"Oh, he'll cooperate. Lock him up. Seth, I believe you have a rendezvous with a damsel in distress."

****

COMMANDER ROBERTS KNOCKED softly on the door to Captain Fielding's temporary quarters on deck four.

"Come in, I've been expecting you," Rea said in a very calm voice, opening the door.

Seth stepped inside and sat down on one of the cushioned chairs. The hint of a sweet smelling perfume filled the room. Rea sat beside him and put her hand on his knee.

"It's been a while since I've seen you," Seth said. "You're looking very well."

Rea smiled. "Thank you."

"You've got to tell me what happened at the Galactic Command inquiry."

Rea's eyes narrowed as she looked at him and began to laugh. "Okay, if that's what you want to talk about...First they separated us and interviewed us individually, and then they brought in Reese. In a nutshell, they didn't believe a word we said, but told us to keep it quiet just in case.

"After we were dismissed, I was stopped at the door by one of the inquiry members and was told that Chance wanted to see me in his quarters, which sounded kind of strange. I had already given my statement, but once there, Chance grilled me about the creature, trying to get more than I had given to the board."

"You're right, there has to be something else he's looking for." Seth leaned back in the soft cushioned chair with a puzzled look on his face.

"You know, I didn't offer you anything to drink or eat. Would you like something?" She started to get up from the chair.

"No, I'm fine. Tell me more about your encounter with Chance." Rea looked at Seth with frustration and sighed. "I told him that the thing destroyed my ship and killed one of my best friends. To those tragic words, he showed no compassion or emotion. I felt very uncomfortable in his presence, as if a cold chill had encircled me."

Rea paused for a moment, then turned away, her mind twisted in a tangle. She wanted to change the subject, but Seth was persistent about talking business. She looked back at Seth and stared into his eyes. "They say the eyes are the window to the soul. Well looking at his, I somehow could tell that something deep and sinister was in the works and it left me with a queasiness in my gut."

Seth nodded. "I sense the same from him."

"Lets not talk about it anymore," she said soothingly. "How about we get some dinner?" She once again put her hand on his knee, this time sliding it up to Seth's mid-thigh. For the first time, he seemed to notice her intentions.

"Fine," replied Seth nervously, "with all that has been going on, I haven't even thought about food. We have a rec lounge that serves up some really good stuff." Rea just laughed.

"So I've heard, and I love stuff. Let's go; I have a big day tomorrow if all the repairs are made on time." She took his hand and they departed from her quarters.

****

A VIEWCOM DISK was delivered to the C & C of Galactic Command. Written on the outside case was the message: *Very important, please view as soon as possible.* He got up from his desk and walked over to his computer station. Taking the disk out of its plastic case, he inserted it into the slot. At that moment the door to the C & C's office slid opened and Chance entered the room.

"Sir, I'm sorry to bother you at this time, but I have the report you requested."

"Thank you Captain, just leave it on my desk." Chance put two viewCOM disks on the C & C's desk.

"Are there any updates on the cloud-creature situation?" asked the Commander & Chief while trying to concentrate on the screen. Chance walked over to see what he was viewing.

"No, there's nothing else, only a few loose ends to tie up," he said. "I think the incidents were just freak accidents with spatial-shifting nebulae. I think those OutStar cowboys got a taste of heroism and wanted more."

Moving closer, Chance saw the shadow of a person on the screen and heard the mystery messenger speak his own name. Chance's expression darkened with fear; a bead of sweat ran down his forehead. He backed up slowly and tried to ease his way out of the C & C's office, but his superior's gaze narrowed as he divided his attention between Chance and the screen. As the shadowy figure continued to speak, the C & C turned up the volume."

"...And I told Chance that if I thought anything was going happen to me or my people, that I would send this transmission to Galactic Command. If this is being read, it means that I have been captured while stealing information for your second in command..."

Chance turned and ran out of C & C's office.

"Damn it, Chance, you're finished here!" the angry Commander & Chief yelled as the sliding door closed behind the traitor. Chance continued to run. Instead of pursuing him personally, the C & C pushed the internal alert button activating the warning lights and sending shrieking alarms throughout the complex. He walked over to the internal COMsystem.

"Attention all security personnel, this is Commander & Chief Vincent Jones speaking. As of this moment Captain Leo J. Chance is no longer a member of the command structure of Galactic Command. He is to be arrested on sight."

Chance, hearing the echo of the C & C's voice reverberating throughout the complex, continued to run down the corridor toward the armory. He pulled out his COMlink and contacted his partners in deception using a special code.

"Be ready for anything. We might have to fight our way out of here. Liant, take two crewmen with you and get the containment chamber that's holding 2LM35."

"Suppose we meet resistance along the way?" Liant responded.

"Don't worry, they don't know you're with me. I'm heading toward the armory now. We will rendezvous in twelve minutes outside the science lab security doors."

****

WITH WEAPONS DRAWN, a small security force led by Captain Rivera searched the complex for Chance.

"Split up into four teams of five and search all corridors, conduits and landing bays," Rivera told his men. "Use whatever force necessary to subdue Chance and anybody who is working with him. Put your weapons on full charge in case you meet any resistance."

****

CHANCE SLOWED DOWN, backed against the wall and peeked his head around the corner, noticing two officers standing guard at the entrance to the armory. Knowing that time was not on his side and that he had nothing to lose at this stage of the game, he jumped out from behind the wall and lunged at top speed, surprising and firing on the first guard. The force of the deadly blast knocked both guards to the ground. Chance disarmed the dead guard, and a proton blast from the other security guard missed his head by mere inches. Before the guard could shoot again, a blast came from Chance's pistol sending the security officer flying backward against the wall and collapsing him in a heap.

Chance got up and overrode the security lock for the weapons room. The doors opened. He had very little time before other security personal would arrive. He snatched a weapons case for his escape. He ran out of the room toward the science lab. As he dashed down the darkened corridor, he was spotted and pursued by three security personnel who continually fired their weapons. Ducking and weaving, the proton blasts hit the corridor walls missing their target. Rounding a corner and with the science lab in view, Chance turned and fired his pistol at the control panel causing a security door to close on the pursuing force, preventing their chase. Continuing on to the science lab, he met up with his men outside the lab doors.

"Sir, when we arrived the doors were locked and the security codes had been changed," one of his men said.

"Don't worry," said Chance. "I have this." From out of his pocket he pulled a small detonation device. "This will override most security lockout systems." The explosive was detonated and the massive doors opened revealing the lab interior. Chance stopped and opened the weapons case.

"Listen up everyone. We don't have much time before they figure out that we've gained access. Take these so that you will remain healthy."

Chance gave the weapons to his loyal henchmen. Chance and his men put the containment chamber that housed the 2LM35 on the antigravity dolly and departed the research lab with the creature.

They quickly moved on, rushing down the corridor that led to the main hangar. Chance spotted an empty scout ship, not knowing that it had just came in for repairs. Security was crawling around the hangar. The men backed up against the wall before they were spotted.

"Listen carefully," he announced softly, "Get down and try to make a run for the scout ship. Move out quickly."

As the twelve men began to move out toward bay two, Chance looked to his right and saw Captain Rivera and his squad running down the corridor."

"Hurry up people! Come on hurry up! Get on board. Secure the creature in the cargo hold and prepare for lift off."

"Chance, hold your position! Don't do this!" Rivera yelled.

"Try to hold this." Chance replied, as he fired his proton pistol at Captain Rivera, just missing him. Another shot coming from his pistol found its mark, downing one of the GC's men.

A barrage of crossfire filled the ship's hangar. Three of Chance's men were down, but still firing. With the rest of his security force diving for cover, Rivera jumped behind the landing strut of another ship and returned the blasts. Chance's men continued the firefight. Blasts from both sides sent debris flying about the hangar.

Rivera, still under the landing strut, fired his pistol continuously, hitting two of Chance's men, propelling them backward into a stack of cargo containers.

Chance ran quickly to the open rear ramp door of the ship, turned and fired his pistol under the ship at Rivera, striking him in the abdomen. Rivera screamed in agony, pulled himself from behind the landing strut and fired one last shot, hitting Chance in the shoulder.

Chance grabbed his shoulder in agony and fired again on Rivera, throwing him back against the dock. Rivera slid down under the ship, lifeless and limp.

Liant, at the scout ship controls, ignited its engines as Chance pushed the button on the rear ramp door activating the closing sequence. Two men from Chance's crew were still pinned down.

"Hurry up! Damn it, we don't have a lot of time. The ramp is being raised."

Both men tried to make a run for it, the first one jumped on the ramp while the other was covering for him. Chance grabbed and pulled in the first man. The second man got up from his covered position and ran, firing at the same time. In desperation, he jumped and managed to grab the top edge of the ramp door, which was halfway closed. Catching a blast in his back, he yelled out in pain. One of the security men knocked him off the door, which closed with a solid thud. Volleys of small arms fire from Rivera's force buffeted the ship's hull, as they tried to disable the craft.

Chance looked out of the viewport and screamed at Liant.

"Initiate emergency lift-off now!" The ship began to rise from its pad using its thrusters to turn and position itself for departure. Rivera's men scattered from their positions to get out of the way of the engine blast.

Liant initiated scout ship's main engines. The ship jolted up, as it spewed an exhaust backwash sending the security guards flying through the hangar into each other and scattering, them like bowling pins.

Soon the ship was well out of range of the security force. Liant set the ship on a course that would take it out of the solar system.

"Damn it!" Chance yelled out, realizing that the ship they had stolen was brought in for repairs.

"Harlan, get in here now."

"What is it sir?"

"Look, I know you've had some electronics experience, so here's what I want you to do. We don't have weapons, long-range tracking or star drive. Do whatever you can to fix them. I don't care how.

Otherwise we will be one huge fireball flaming across the cosmos. Galactic Command isn't going to just sit by and just let us waltz out of here."

A tense ten minutes went by before Chance was contacted by the C & C via the ship's viewCOM.

"Chance, turn the craft around. There is nowhere you can go that I won't find you. As it stands now you face charges of murder, assault and theft of GC property, not to mention conspiracy. If you return without putting up a fight, I might be able to have some of the charges dismissed or reduced, but remember that it will still be under TESSA's jurisdiction. Don't make me have to destroy you."

Chance shrugged without saying a word as the Commander & Chief continued.

"As I'm speaking to you, there's an attack force leaving Galactic Command with the orders to destroy you on sight if you do not surrender. Your ship isn't capable of defending itself from a small meteor. Turn back now."

Chance turned off the screen and Harlan approached him.

"Sir, we now have long range tracking and I think I got star drive working."

Chance smiled. "Good work, but now we also have Galactic battle cruisers on an intercept course with an ETA of nineteen minutes and closing."

"The automatic sensors that link up to the motors of the weapons systems are badly damaged, however, the weapons can still be fired and aimed manually," Harlan said.

"Well done, Harlan," said Chance, sounding relieved. "Let's go to star drive to put some distance between us and them, and I want you to take this and link it up with the ship's engines." Chance slid open a recessed panel, reached in, pulled out a large circuit board and handed it to Harlan. "Behind the star drive computer system you'll find a slot that will accept the board I just gave you. Put it in and then notify me when you've completed the task." Harlan recognized the unit as a power conversion booster.

"Once we are ready for star drive we will prepare a little surprise for the pursuing ships in case they try to track us. If what I have in mind works, they will not be able to determine our course. Drain some of the hydrazine from the star drive core and put it into two of those large self-contained pressure containers that I spotted when we entered this ship."

"That is a very dangerous idea, but it could work, and I don't see any other option."

"Well, what the hell are you standing around for? Do it, and do it quickly, before we are detected. Move it!" yelled Chance.

Harlan and two crewmembers left the cockpit, leaving Chance alone until the work was done. As Chance and his crew continued to hurtle through the vastness of space, the battle cruisers deployed by Galactic Command continued to hunt him down.

****

ALONE AND FRUSTRATED the Commander and Chief sat in his dimly lit quarters and thought to himself, *Where did I go wrong? I trusted that bastard with everything.*

****

VOICES CAME OVER the internal COMsystem of one of the GC battle cruisers in pursuit of the renegade Chance.

"Battle alert! All senior officers to the command center. We have picked up the identification code of the scout ship and have him on our long-range screen. At present speed, we will be in firing range in less then three minutes."

The scout ship's proximity alert system sounded automatically as it picked up the battle cruisers' identification code, alerting Chance that the two ships were closing in on him. Chance's frantic voice and image came over the COMsystem. "I can see them! Are we ready? GC ships are practically on us. We can't let them get too close."

"Ready. How the hell are we going to release these things?" asked Harland, carrying the containers of hydrazine.

"Put them in the ventilation shaft," answered Chance.

"Me?"

"Yes you. Do it now! At this point every second counts."

Harlan opened the inner hatch of the ventilation shaft. He and one other crewmen carefully placed the two containers, one behind the other, inside the shaft, and closed the inner hatch door. Through the ship's COMsystem he announced to Chance that they were ready.

The two GC battle cruisers commenced firing on the renegade ship. The scout ship, with Liant still at the controls, managed to evade GC's proton blasts by using quick pitch and roll maneuvers, but it was still being shaken up. Tensions mounted. The captains of the battle cruisers prepared to fire long-range power-seeking proton missiles.

An alarm sounded, indicating the scout ship that the missiles had locked onto their position. Chance began to monitor distance and speed on his strategic viewscreen.

"Missiles bearing six hundred-five point eight; distance, fourteen miles; speed, Mach three point five. Damn it, I hope this works. Everybody stay alert, this is going to be close."

"Vent shaft pressurized," Harlan panted.

Sweat began to pour from Chance — he knew that one mistake could cost them their lives. Chance began the distance countdown to launch countermeasures.

"Distance, Eight point nine miles, seven point three miles, five point seven miles."

"What the hell are you waiting for, Chance, tell me to launch these things!" Harlan shouted, with a sweaty left hand gripping the release lever.

"Shut up and stay focused. Four point nine miles and closing, three point seven miles; their missiles are armed and rigged for structural impact, distance two point two miles, launch counter measures... now." The vent shaft hatch opened and the two hydrazine containers were sucked out into the vacuum of space.

"Weapons crewman, move from your console now! Move!" The man jumped up from his chair, tripping over his own feet and falling to the floor. Chance moved to the station, looked down at the targeting scope and fired two proton bursts at the containers causing an explosion that attracted the missiles, which burst forth in a hot, white flash. Chance yelled to Liant to engage maximum star drive.

The two battle cruisers tried to evade the rippling explosion, but got caught in the outer edge of the gravimetrical waves, causing them to loose their tracking capabilities for five seconds. But that five seconds was more than enough time for Chance to disappear in a cluster of stars at full star drive.

10

REJOINING FORCES

"We have Commander & Chief Vincent Jone on viewCOM for you, Chief," said Roberts, as the doors of the command center slid open to reveal Chief Mack and Captain Jones.

"Chief Mack, it's good to see you again."

"Likewise, Commander & Chief. We have some information that may interest you." The C & C looked down. Gritting his teeth, he answered in a solemn voice.

"I have some very disturbing news, as well. Chance has turned renegade and has managed to steal one of our scout ships. He has also stolen the containment unit that housed the alien you captured. From what I've learned, it seems that he may have figured out a way to communicate with the thing. At this point, I'd say that he's become very dangerous and unpredictable."

"Wait a minute!" said the chief, "He's gone? Get Code in here. He will have answers."

"What are you talking about? the C & C asked.

"We captured a Stealth breaking into our computer lab. He confessed to working for Chance. And he can communicate with the cloud creature…he has been for quite some time."

"I don't understand."

"The cloud creatures are highly intelligent nanocons that are kidnapping human children for genetic experiments."

"This is more than I can fathom, Wingate. Chance is selling out his own people and their children. For what? Money?"

"Lots of money. And power. His position makes him very valuable to them. Safe and valuable."

"Very well, I will alert TESSA and begin an inquiry. If he shows up, contact me immediately. We have contracted Mier Salvage to bring back what's left of the battle cruiser that was destroyed by the alien."

"Commander & Chief, have Captain Rivera contact me about tactics. He knows Chance's patterns better than anyone."

"I'm sorry, Chief, Captain Rivera was seriously injured attempting to prevent Chance's escape and is in critical condition. We don't know if he will make it."

****

Captain Rea Fielding's ship was moving through space at a moderate speed on her way back to Comet Impact Supply Company. One of her crew noticed an object on the deep space scanner.

"Rea, I'm picking up something on my scanner. It could be a ship on an intercept course." Rea sat down at her post and punched up a log of vessels that the company did business with and saw nothing scheduled. "We are not scheduled to meet any ships from our company or any other company."

"Captain, the vessel is getting closer, but I still can't get a clear identification code lock. Their code seems to be jammed as if they don't want to be detected." Fielding moved over to her crewmate to see for herself.

"Well, what type of vessel is it?" asked Rea, leaning over her coworker's shoulder and peering into the viewscreen.

"Got it!" said the crewmember. "Definitely Galactic Command's design configuration. It's a scout ship."

Rea sensed that something was wrong when she looked through the forward cockpit window out into space.

"What's the weapons status of that ship?" yelled Rea. Suddenly, the scout ship's cannons fired two proton bursts. The bursts traveled at great speed and narrowly missed the defenseless freighter. The two bursts exploded in close proximity but nothing was damaged. The crew tried to hold on to whatever supports they could as the ship rocked from the concussion.

Rea struggled over to the viewCOM in shock, wondering why a Galactic Command scout ship would attack a freighter. She signaled the vessel and the transmission was indicated as received.

"Who the hell are you and why did you fire on us? We are an unarmed freighter." A face with a sinister smile appeared on the viewCOM.

"Hello Rea. How are you today?"

"You slimy son of a bitch, why have you attacked us?" screamed Rea, recognizing the cold, evil stare of Leo J. Chance.

"Look who's calling who a bitch," Chance said with a sly look and voice that cut through the crew like a sharp knife. "Look ladies, I need supplies and it looks like you have what I need."

One of the crewmembers grabbed Fielding by the shoulder.

"Captain, what the hell is going on? Is this man crazy or something?"

"You don't know the half of it. If we get out of this, I'll explain the whole thing to you."

"Look, I don't have any supplies on board. I just left OutStar One after emergency repairs were made to this freighter."

Disbelief and anger emanated from Chance's face.

"I don't want to talk anymore," he said impatiently. "Prepare to be boarded or..." Chance paused, "...or you know what will happen. Those first shots were just a warning."

"Well I suggest you prepare yourself. This bitch does not go down with out a fight." Knowing that the freighter couldn't outrun the scout ship, Rea, moved to the pilot's seat and looked around at panic in her crewmates' faces.

The two ships continued toward one another at high speed, rapidly closing the distance between them on an intercept course. Chance's ship continued to fire its weapons manually, rocking Fielding's freighter with near misses. Electronic malfunction alarms began to appear on the workstations in her command center.

"Why aren't they locking on us?" Rea muttered to herself.

"They should've locked on by now," one of the crewmembers interjected. Maybe their locking capability is down."

"Well, if you're right, we should all thank our maker for this one."

"Captain! Are we going to die?"

Rea was angry. "Not if I can help it!"

As the two ships got closer, Chance yelled at Liant.

"What the hell is going on? We haven't hit her yet! Fire, fire!"

"I'm trying, but we have a problem."

"What problem?" asked Chance.

"We've lost proton control and the firing coils are overheating."

Chance moved over to the fire control panel and pounded on the firing buttons with his fist, attempting to reactivate the system but to no avail. Liant monitored the range meter.

"Sir, may I remind you that that ship is less than six hundred thousand meters away. She's much larger than us and, according to the navigational computer, her present course is constant bearing, decreasing range...sir, I think she intends to ram us." Chance rushed over to the station manned by Liant to see for himself.

"That bitch is crazy. Hard to port, hard to port... now!" yelled Chance. As the massive star freighter was about to impact the much smaller scout ship, Liant executed Chance's evasive maneuver and at the last second veered out of harm's way. Chance established contact with Fielding.

"Listen you crazy fool. You don't know how lucky you are. If I had the time, I'd chase you down and finish you off, but I have other pressing matters. There will be another time." Transmission was aborted and the scout ship continued on into deep space.

****

CHANCE WAS AT his wit's end. It was time to contact the nanocons.

"Liant, get 4SB73 on viewCOM."

"Yes, Captain."

In a moment, the pulsating cloud-like being was on the viewscreen with translator activated.

"So, you made it out alive, did you? Good for you."

"Barely, 4SB73. Our ship is in bad shape. We'll need to rendezvous very soon."

"I don't know why we should help you. You can offer us no more protection from Galactic Command. You got sloppy, Chance."

"It was that damn OutStar crew. I have been very loyal to you. You have to help us."

"Fine, I will hold up my end of our bargain and, if your clunker of a ship can make it, we will meet you on The Ecliptic World in two days. Make sure you keep Galactic Command away. Don't let us down, Chance, or else "

****

Rea Fielding contacted Seth Roberts via his personal viewCOM in his quarters.

"I see you made it back safely, that's good news," Seth beamed, happy to hear from her.

"I almost didn't."

"Did you have some kind of mechanical problem?"

"No, I happened to run into Chance and he almost killed me and my crew."

"Are you okay?" Seth's voice betrayed his internal panic.

"Only some minor cuts and bruises from being rocked about by his fire power. He barely missed us."

"Thank God you're alive. Do you know where he was headed?"

"We tracked him heading in the direction of the Canas Major system."

"The Ecliptic World—we have it under authority that the nanocons will strike there next. Did you contact Galactic Command and inform them of what happened to you?"

"Yes I did. They said they would divert several ships to that area hoping to pick up his ship's signature using extended sensor rangefinders. They also told me that because of his tactical background and training, not to get too excited about finding him.

It's going to be like trying to find a needle in ten thousand light-years of space, but it's not impossible."

"How did you get away? What was his weapons status?"

Before Seth could ask any more questions, Rea snapped back.

"I'd love to keep talking shop, since that's all that interests you, but my crew and I have been ordered to medical to undergo examinations before we report back to work. Unfortunately, I won't be seeing much of you in the near future so take care of yourself. Don't worry about to finding me, I'll find you." Rea ended the transmission.

11

Paradise

THE CANAS MAJOR GALAXY PRESENTED a vision of strange, varicolored nebulae filling the sky. Beautiful star fields opened up before the OutStar as it came out of star drive approaching The Ecliptic World. Looking through the view ports, the crew could see the moons that nightly produced a spectacular eclipse that made this planet such a popular vacation destination throughout the system.

Tourists came from all over, mingling with the people who lived and worked there. The OutStar moved within sensor range and was picked up by the tower on Capital One, the biggest and most populated colony on The Ecliptic World.

As a reward for their hard work and to unwind from their recent traumas, Chief Mack ordered three days of rest and rejuvenation for his colleagues. While the pre-vacation meeting was still in session, a young ensign notified Chief Mack that an incoming viewCOM signal was coming from Capital One. Wingate quietly left the meeting and walked over to the viewCOM. He pushed a button to activate the screen. "

"This is Capital One on The Ecliptic World. We have you on approach scan. Please identify yourself."

"This is Chief Operations Officer Wingate Mack of OutStar One. With whom am I speaking?"

"Sir, you are speaking with tower controller Kord, and may I say we are glad to see you made it safely. The General Director wants to greet you and your crew personally when you land."

"Thank you, Mr. Kord. We are looking forward to a lovely vacation."

"Chief, do you have two ships or one?"

"Why do you ask? Is there a problem?"

"At this time we can only accommodate one ship. All the other landing pads are occupied."

"Don't worry," said the chief. "We have two ships but will be coming in as one." Kord looked puzzled. "You'll see what I mean when we get there," the chief said, as he recorded the instructions for the flight path.

"You can come in on 83178 north by 14828 west and land on pad two."

The chief thanked Kord, ended the transmission and turned to his crew.

"Well, folks, we will be landing on Capitol One shortly."

A rush of excitement rippled through the gathering. The cheers of the crew on their way out of the cargo bay surprised even the chief. As the crew left the bay area, the officers took their positions in the secondary command center to enable the separation sequence.

Commander Roberts contacted the main ship and told the lead flight officer to make ready for release and to monitor the countdown.

"By the way who is the lead flight officer?"

"Sir, you are talking to her," Lt. Martinez said with a smile in her voice. "Is there a problem?"

"No, just wondering who was in command up there. Okay Lieutenant, there will be a fifteen second countdown before separation, on my mark starting…

now. Lieutenant, stand by for vertical thruster ignition once separation is achieved."

"Mr. Roberts, I'm well aware of vertical thruster operation. This is not my first separation." Seth turned to face Wingate and Jack.

"Is she always like this?" Both men laughed to themselves. Seth turned in the opposite direction to face Anjum.

"Okay, Anjum, prepare to release the strut doors and disengage the magnetic field in eleven seconds, ten..." The strut doors opened; the magnetic field was disengaged. The main ship activated its vertical lift thrusters and pulled away from the cargo section to give itself some distance.

"Okay Anjum, follow the flight path instructions from the Capitol One tower control and take us in nice and easy," Wingate interjected as both ships descended into the atmosphere of The Ecliptic World. Turbulent crosswinds rocked the ships.

"I'll try to make it a smooth ride, but according to our weather tracking monitor and from what we are feeling right now, there will be a bit of a rough ride ahead of us. Hopefully, it won't last long," Anjum said.

The chief looked down at his monitor, "Anjum, what's happening to our speed?"

"Judging from our gravitational pull meters, this planet has twelve and a half percent less gravitational pull than Earth does. This gives us a slight advantage on descent and vector status."

Both ships continued to descend through the cloudy atmosphere at three-quarter thruster power. The main ship followed the payload section at a distance of about one point two kilometers, both ships feeling the effects of turbulence as they descended. Finally breaking through cloud cover, the city of Capitol One, lit by the afternoon sun, filled the viewscreens.

"Anjum, what happened to that smooth ride that we were supposed to have? My stomach feels like it's in my mouth!"

"Sorry Chief, the turbulence had other ideas."

"Don't you think someone should start to lower the landing struts?" Jack interjected. "Or should we just land on our belly?"

"Very funny, Jack, go ahead. Engage landing sequence."

The payload section closed in on Capital One's landing port. The distance was five kilometers to touchdown when Kord contacted them.

"I have you on final approach." Looking at his tracking scope, Kord paused briefly as his eyes widened and his expression changed to panic.

"Where did that other ship come from?" His voice echoed around the tower getting the attention of the other flight controllers who crowded around him to see what was going on.

"OS One, I see an unauthorized ship following your flight path, distance about two kilometers and closing. I'm going to try to wave it off. That ship does not have flight clearance."

"Mr. Kord, this is Chief Mack of OutStar One. That ship is part of us. Please disengage any emergency protocols."

"How is it part of your ship?" Kord asked.

"Don't worry, you'll see what I mean."

The payload section was coming in on a slight angle but leveled off over landing pad number two. The huge ship slowed down and hovered over the landing pad with thrusters at half power, ready to touch down on its struts and made a soft landing on the pad followed by the main ship, which landed on top of the payload section. Both ships cut power.

"What a ride! I hope everything is still intact and everybody is OK," the chief said.

Anjum received a signal from the main ship letting him know that the landing struts were properly secured in their channels and ready for lock-down. He reactivated the strut doors and re-engaged the magnetic locks that held the main ship in place.

"Well, gentlemen," Seth said. "It seems we have arrived in one piece and I know I can't wait to set foot on this soil."

"I am going to enjoy this, too. I really need a vacation after the ordeals we've all been through and after spending so much time trying to keep you guys healthy," Dr. Mutara laughed.

"You deserve it, Doctor," the chief said, "and so does the rest of the crew. Now we all can unwind and enjoy our time off. I hear the eclipse is exhilarating."

Win and the others went down to meet the General Director. The main ship flight crew, headed by Lt. Jessica Martinez, joined them in the payload section. After about five minutes, the main ramp door was activated and dropped down to rest on the pad.

Chief Mack, Dr. Mutara, Lt. Commander Anjum Sarwar, Captain Jack Jones, Commander Seth Roberts, Lt. Tapia Tunica and Lt. Jessica Martinez walked down the ramp. When they reached the bottom they noticed a crowd in the distance waiting to greet them.

"What's this? A welcoming committee?" asked Jack. Anjum looked surprised.

"I don't know. I guess we will find out soon enough."

A man of small build, but with a aura of importance and accompanied by security personnel walked up to greet the officers of OS One.

"I'm General Director Quest Fay and I would like to welcome you and your crew to Capital One."

Chief Mack shook his hand, feeling the grip of a confident man.

"I'm Chief Wingate Mack, operations officer of this ship and these are my officers and crew. May I say we are glad to be of service to you and your colony."

"What's the story with all those people?" Seth asked. Fay turned his head and chuckled.

"Well, I suppose you don't know it, but you're still the talk of the galaxy. These people have all come out to see the famous OutStar One and her gallant crew. Frankly, I'm excited to see you myself, as well as honored."

Fay cast his eyes upon the smooth, ebony skin of Doctor Mutara and nervously shook her hand, gripping it tightly.

"Pleased to meet you, madam, do enjoy your stay. If there's anything I can do for you, just let me know." Mutara flashed a smile at him. Captain Jones watched the interchange with interest.

"There is something you can do for me at the moment."

"What is it?"

"Please let go of my hand, thank you." Jack smiled.

"Oh...Oh I'm terribly sorry. Please forgive me."

He let go of the doctor's hand and led the officers toward the landing area exit gate. General Director Fay turned and pointed.

"At the Colony Inn, you will find a lovely restaurant and amenities if you need a break from your ship." As they went through the gate, Quest asked a question.

"I'm curious about something. Why do you use a military chain of command to run your business?"

"I found it more efficient than using the words 'boss' or 'supervisor' and it works so well with Galactic Command."

Quest Fay nodded his head in agreement but was interrupted by a signal from his COMlink.

"Excuse me, Chief." Before it could signal a third time he removed it from his belt, pushed a button and began talking with one of his security people. The chief noticed a group of about fifteen children of different ages and different planetary nationalities looking in his direction. He waved politely and the children laughed and ran off to play. Quest Fay finished his conversation

"Chief, I'm needed in the administration building. I think you can find your way around here, but if not, our people are very friendly and will be happy to assist you and your crew. I'm sorry I can't accompany you right now, but I'm sure I'll see you later." He turned and walked away in a hurry through another exit gate.

****

THE MAIN CREW sat at a wide, round table, on a spacious sixth level patio at the Colony Inn overlooking the beautiful city enjoying delicious, local vegetables and fruits from the hydroponics garden on the premises. They noticed the moons and their splendid colors in the late afternoon sky that would eventually converge to create the magnificent eclipse—the major attraction of Capital One.

"I can't believe the freshness of this food," Seth said. "It's better than fresh. I just can't describe it."

"Well, enjoy it while you can. We are going to be very busy when we get back to the ship," said Anjum, narrowing his gaze at Tapia who just smiled and nodded her head in a 'yes' gesture. Win looked at Jack who seemed to be preoccupied with something.

"Jack what's the matter? You seem to be elsewhere." Jack leaned back in the cushioned chair

"I've got a bad feeling in the pit of my stomach."

"What do you mean? Are you coming down with something? Should I call the doctor over?"

"No, I'm not sick, and I know I shouldn't feel this way in this place of exhilarating beauty. It's more of an eerie feeling, as if something bad is in the air." His head tilted up to the sky as if searching for something.

"I can sense what you're feeling, Captain. Sometimes my dreams are disturbed with visions and feelings I can't understand. But I do know something is not right here."

****

THE FIRST TWO days on Capital One were like a dream come true for the three hundred-member crew of OutStar One. They witnessed the most fantastic colorful display in the galaxy. An eclipse of nine moons lined up like a string of pearls, blocking out the sun many millions of miles away every thirty-six hours, as a myriad of colors flashed between them. For the crew, this was the first time in a long time that they were able to really enjoy themselves.

Day three arrived on Capitol One. Tourists moved around the city and its outskirts, taking in the beautiful vistas and in the middle of all of this splendor, children played in the open plaza, a place where people from around the system gathered to watch the eclipse, enjoy foods sold by street vendors, listen to music and buy souvenirs for friends and relatives back home.

It was 15:00 hours. Streams of red and blue light poked through the colored clouds as the sun beamed down creating an angelic bath of light across the land. With a gentle breeze blowing through Capitol One, the day was perfect. The gorgeous birds that flew overhead were indigenous to the planet and were not dangerous, but kept mostly to themselves while avoiding the aerial traffic that taxied people to different parts of Capitol One.

As the day moved on, perched on the ramp door of the OutStar, Tapia leaned against one of the side rails checking the incoming job request log. There were at least nine survey jobs pending. Hearing footsteps coming behind her, she turned around and saw Captain Jones.

"I see you have the request log," said Jack. "How much work did we get?"

"We have enough to keep us busy for a while," said Tapia, handing it over.

"Wow, the chief is going to like this. By the way, where is Wingate?"

Tapia thought for a moment and then turned to point in the direction of the plaza.

"I think he and some of the crew went to the plaza to enjoy the festivities and to watch the eclipse as it develops. This is our last day on this planet paradise so we better enjoy it."

"What say we join him and the others while we can?"

"Let's go," Tapia said. They walked down the ramp door and headed for the plaza to see if they could find the others.

"I'm going to see if I can find a gift for my father, if you don't mind," said the captain.

"Not at all. If I can't find you later on, I'll see you on board the OutStar at 21:00 hours for departure. Don't get lost," she sing-songed.

"No problem" said the captain as he peeled off and walked toward the vendors and shops.

Tapia moved through the crowd to see if she could find the chief. She bumped into a crewmember holding a skewer of exotic meats in his left hand.

"Have you seen the Win or Seth?" asked Tapia. Before taking another bite, he pointed in the direction of the plaza.

"Yes, I think they are watching some kids play a game."

"Really?" asked Tapia.

"You'll find them and a big crowd of people watching the game."

Tapia reminded the crewman about the departure time and continued on her search. The sun star was still beaming down its rays in the late afternoon as the crowd began to look up to view the convergence of the moons.

****

IN THE LANDING-PORT tower something strange appeared on Kord's monitor. It did not fit any of the ship configurations listed in the computer identification logs. He thought perhaps his instruments needed realignment, so he ran a diagnostic test, only to find that everything was running properly.

Concerned, he called over three other controllers to see if they had seen anything like the nebulous object appearing on his scope. They all shook their heads.

"Whatever that is, it seems to be huge, the size of five giant starships," said controller Park.

"Where the hell is it landing?" asked Ips.

Kord measured the distance on the scope. "It's setting down way out on the outer rim, some distance away from the city. I don't like it."

"Well, what are we going to do?" asked Bost.

"The only thing we can do is contact Quest Fay, give him the approximate coordinates of this thing and let him send somebody out there to take a look," Kord offered. The other controllers agreed and went back to monitoring their own stations. Fay was contacted and sent an emergency team to check out the disturbance.

****

TAPIA, FOLLOWING THE noise from the crowd, found the chief and the others watching the native children playing a game. The convergence of the nine moons started as the first moon began to block out the sun's rays, creating a dark shadow that slowly swept across Capital One. As the sun became eclipsed, the other moons lined up, one behind the other, like soldiers. The eclipse stopped the game as everyone in the city and its environs turned their attentions to the show in the heavens. The excited hydrogen emissions between each moon created a kaleidoscope of bright colors that glowed with a star-like effect as they moved into position. Even the birds stopped in their flight to look up at the only place in the known galaxy that could put on such a show. It would be three hours before the moons would begin to separate, as if they had slowly danced together and then parted ways to find another partner.

✷✷✷✷✷✷✷✷✷✷✷✷✷✷

IN ONE OF the meeting rooms Quest Fay and his security and administrative personnel discussed what could have gone wrong with the emergency team that was sent to investigate the unauthorized landing.

"Damn it, why they haven't reported in? They know the procedure," said an angry Quest Fay, jumping up from his chair and slamming his fist down on the large conference table. "Does anybody have any ideas as to why we haven't heard anything?"

"Yes," said one of the communications personnel leaning forward in his chair. "Sir, sometimes communication is garbled in mountain areas due to metal deposits."

"Did they arm themselves before they left?"

"No, they took just the usual scanning equipment," said the security officer.

****

OUTSIDE, THE WEATHER began to change. The winds whipped around in different directions. A sweet smell wafted through the winds as they picked up strength. The inhabitants on Capitol One looked around trying to pinpoint from where the smell was coming. The odor intensified to the point of becoming almost intoxicating, adding to the prevailing excitement as the moons moved away from one another into their own elliptical orbits, breaking the pearl effect.

With the sun setting in the western hemisphere, the moons that covered it slowly moved away, restoring some light to Capitol One, but not for long.

As the natural darkness set in, the glow of artificial lights illuminated the plaza, the walkways and the large complexes that made up Capitol One.

"Wow! What a show! What a show!" exclaimed Captain Jones, who was still watching the moons.

"Yeah, my wife and son would have loved this," said the chief, starting to feel a little depressed while gazing into the heavens. Tapia turned and tapped the chief on the shoulder getting his attention.

"Yes, what is it?" said the chief turning his head to see what she wanted.

"I just wanted to remind you that we have orders to…" the chief cut her off in mid-sentence.

"Yes, I know about the orders. It's just, well, you know what I mean, this place is like something out of a dream." Tapia smiled and nodded her head in agreement.

12

Paradise Lost

FAR BEHIND THE Monolith Mountains on the outer rim of The Ecliptic World, the cloud creatures dispatched by 4SB73 prepared to pillage Capitol One. The first team of investigators, unfortunately, had become the first victims of the horror.

In the flight tower, Kord checked out the last coordinates where he had monitored the landing. Looking at the bright blue transport-tracking screen, his eyes caught something moving, but where once there was only one strange object, now there were many, and all converging on Capitol One. His whole body tightened as if caught in a vise.

"What the hell are they?" he yelled getting the attention of the other flight controllers.

"What's wrong?" yelled Park, turning from his screen to look in Kord's direction.

"Get over here, quick. You have to see this." Park leaned over Kord's shoulder to view the screen.

"Wait a minute!" said Park, pointing at the lower section of the screen. His eyes widened in nervous wonder. "Is that the same thing we saw earlier?"

"Yes it is," replied Kord.

"But…but, we saw only one, now there are, wait, eight of those things moving towards us."

****

IN THE PLAZA, the crowd began to disperse. As people left the plaza, it was easy for the crew of the OutStar to find one another.

"Well kids," said the chief, throwing up his hands in the air.

"Please don't say it, we all know what it means," Jack cut in. Everyone nodded in agreement. As they walked out of the plaza, Tapia stopped.

"Stop everyone."

"What's wrong?" asked Jessica.

"Something's up," exclaimed Jack.

Tapia folded her hands together and closed her eyes, letting her natural hyper-senses take over.

Everyone remained quiet as not to distract her. With her eyes still closed and her respiration becoming rapid, she began to talk and gesture with her hands.

"There's something moving this way, I can barely make it out." Jack and Win looked at each other. Her eyes snapped opened and her respiration returned to normal.

"I see the Chelsea colony," Tapia said.

****

THE ARMY OF deadly interstellar life-forms neared Capitol One, but this time, unlike the Chelsea attack, it had split into more than twenty beings, each one as huge and deadly as the one from which it separated.

"Did you feet that?" asked Dr. Mutara, as the ground shook beneath their feet.

"Yes, I think we all did," replied Seth.

"We should contact Quest Fay," Jessica thought out loud.

"We'll contact Mr. Fay when we get back to the ship," said Jack.

"Ok, let's go," replied the chief. They all turned and continued on toward the ship.

As they reached the landing-port entrance, the ground trembled again. They looked at each other.

A loud emergency siren went off. Its sound was heard all over Capitol One.

"That sounds like an emergency signal!" shouted Seth. They looked behind them and saw hundreds of panicked people and children running in terror. Shouts came up from the crowd.

"There's something coming! There's something coming!"

"It's them, it has to be them," said Seth.

"Chief, we have to help these people in anyway we can," Anjum said excitedly.

"Yes, I know. Let's get to the OutStar."

Rushing through the entrance gate, they saw the work crew standing at the bottom of the ramp to the ship.

"We are under attack by the same creatures that destroyed the Chelsea colony," Chief Mack informed his people.

"Well, what are we to do?" asked one of the men.

"Has everyone reported to base and boarded the ship?" asked Seth.

"No, most of them still have not reported," replied the crewman.

"OK, here's what we are going to do. Get as many people—civilian, crew, everyone, on board and ready both ships for emergency lift-off."

"OK, Chief, I'm on it," responded the crewman, as he motioned the others to follow him inside the OutStar. The chief turned to confront his officers.

"Seth, I want you to break out the proton pistols and distribute them to whomever will go with me. Let's see if we can kill these things or at least slow them down enough to give the Ecliptian people a chance to get on board the OutStar or get out of Capitol One and into the mountains. Who's with me?" the chief asked looking at the faces of his trusted friends.

"Come on, Wingate, you already know the answer to that question," said Jack. "We been through this before. There is no turning back now."

Tapia, Anjum, Odette, Seth and Jessica looked on in agreement.

"Well, what are we waiting for? Lets move!" said the chief as they moved quickly up the ramp door and into the ship.

On the landing docks, all hell was breaking loose. The commercial and cruise ships that occupied most of the landing pads in the port began to lift off, trying to get away from the approaching danger. The officers of OutStar One exited their ship with proton pistols at the ready. As they moved through the gate, the noise of people screaming and running was deafening. In the distance, flashes of light mingled with rising smoke against the dark sky and the strange unearthly hum of the cloud creatures overtook the screams of the citizens of Capitol One.

Doctor Mutara grabbed the chief's shoulder and stopped him.

"Doctor, what's wrong?"

"I'm going back to gather my medical staff and set up a trauma area."

"Great idea, Doctor." the chief said. "Here, you better take this." The doctor took his proton pistol and held it at arm's length. "No, really, you'd better keep it, in case those things reach this far."

The doctor was silent for a moment, as she looked at Win, Jack and the rest of the crew, wondering if she would ever see them again.

"I know that look, Doctor. Try not to worry. If we can't fight them off, we will get back in time for our own escape," said the chief.

"OK, but please be careful," said the doctor as she turned and started back towards the OutStar. With their weapons raised, the OutStar One crew forced their way through the crowds of hysterical people trying frantically to find a safe haven from the onslaught that was turning Capitol One into rubble.

Jack spotted an abandoned aerial taxi with its doors wide-open and its rotary engines still winding in idle mode. He signaled the others.

"We got one, over here! Come on, let's go." They piled in, Seth took the controls and moved the throttle control from its standby position to hover-mode. The engine whined, lifted the craft to about thirty-five meters and sped off in the direction of the destructive forces.

When they reached the other side of Capital One, Seth landed the craft short of a destroyed office building. The putrid stench of smoke mixed with death filled their nostrils. They choked and gasped for air, as they affixed their toxin-filtration masks. Despite the warm 70-degree night air, they shivered with foreboding. The team stopped dead in its tracks, each member's eyes bulging in their sockets. It was worse than they could imagine.

Moving down the wide street between the tall buildings were five giant smoke creatures, one behind the other. A blue haze enveloped the black thick smoke that floated where the creatures had been. Buildings lay in ruin and electrical fires and small explosions flared at random.

Aerial taxis containing charred, shriveled bodies lay scattered among the debris of what used to be a communication center. The pavement cracked and gave way under the intense heat the creatures emitted. Long octopus-like tentacles reached and searched for anything moving inside the breached buildings. A group of colonists, who had survived falling debris, dashed out from an opening and began to run toward the OutStar One crew.

"Help! Help!" they screamed. But one of the creatures' hyper-senses picked up on the survivors and with a quick whip of its tentacles, it reached out and grabbed hold of four children and one adult male. They screamed wildly and hysterically, as the children were dragged across the broken pavement and into the nucleus of the creature where they vanished.

The OutStar One crew moved in synchronicity as their proton blasts found their mark. The blast flared out on impact as if there was some sort of shield preventing the blast from entering inside the smoke creature. Undeterred, it moved forward and dragged the man into the darkness of its nucleus.

"They're too big this time! Go for the tentacles!"

They trained their weapons on the long tentacles and opened fire. As each blast found its mark, the creature recoiled with a loud shriek, as if it had been stung. Letting go of its prey, it retracted the tentacles back inside its core. But they were too late. The charred carcass of the man fell to the ground with a thud.

"I'm going to get the rest of them. Cover me!" Jack said

"Be careful. Those things have a good twenty-meter reach," shouted Win as Tapia, Anjum, Seth and

Jessica began laying down blast after blast to keep the other creatures distracted. Within seconds, Jack reached the remaining two kids, scooped them up in one movement with outstretched arms.

The creature sensed the movement and extended its long deadly tentacles toward the fleeing captain and his two young survivors, but was stopped again by proton blasts and retracted its tentacles.

Jack passed the children off to a group of survivors huddled in a doorway. Anjum directed them to an aerial taxi parked down the street about six blocks away and told them to wait there. Taking Anjum's advice, the survivors ran in the direction of the taxi and were soon out of sight of the OutStar crew.

The blue haze surrounding the injured creature shot out in rays to the other creatures behind it, linking them. They stopped moving as the conjoined blue haze began to pulsate and glow with intensity bright enough to light the area around them.

"What the hell are they doing now?" asked Tapia.

"That beam, if I were to guess, is a form of communication," Seth offered.

"They might be coming up with a plan," Anjum remarked.

"Look, we've got to get out of here before those things start moving again," said Tapia as she tugged on Win's shoulder desperately. The chief relented.

"Let's get the hell out of here."

They backed out at a quick pace, keeping their proton pistols at the ready and their eyes glued on the creatures. Without warning, a lightning-like blast shot out from the creatures directly at the OutStar One crew. It struck the ground with a hot flash just missing Jack. Blast after blast followed in rapid succession.

"Move! Move! Move!" shouted the chief as they ran, returning fire. They ducked behind a small building and leaned against the wall.

"Well, I'll be damned, Seth remarked. "Those things are smart; they analyzed what we did and used it against us."

"I hear an aerial taxi. Who the hell could that be?" frowned Win, looking up at the bright lights descending a short distance away.

"Look, it's Quest Fay," said Jack.

The General Director landed the taxi and ran to the assembled OS crew. He was panic-stricken and spoke so quickly, it was hard to understand him.

"Kord informs me that those things have broken off into twenty or more entities and are surrounding Capitol One and are closing in like a noose around our necks. We've got to do something about this situation. We have to fight off whatever those things are. The corporations that built this colony spent lots of money and time and to develop and promote one of the most attractive sights in the galaxy and they may not be able to rebuild what we have here." They all stared at Quest Fay.

"Since you haven't noticed it pal, I'll point out that there are people dying all around you," said Jack angrily.

Quest Fay hung his head, breaking eye contact with the crew.

"Look, we understand your dilemma, but this is a war. We will stay to the bitter end and save as many people as we can, but we need your help."

Everyone nodded in agreement with the chief and made a run for the two aerial taxis. Quest Fay called for his civilian patrol to take their positions around the city.

From the taxis, at a height of about thirty meters, the OutStar crew looked down and saw panicked people running in terror, not knowing which way to turn. The Civilian Guard attempted to herd the citizens toward the landing port. Reaching their destination just outside of the landing port, the two taxis descended slowly and came to rest, shutting down their engines.

Quest Fay exited his transport with the survivors and yelled out, "chief, you go ahead. I'll get these people out on my shuttle."

"OK," replied the chief. Quest Fay turned and was soon out of sight with the survivors in tow.

Aware of each frantic movement of life around them, Seth rallied his team

"Come on, come on! Every second counts." They followed his lead and ran toward the entrance gate. Work crews and security personnel loaded as many people as they could onto OS One.

In the confusion of the battle, the renegade scout ship led by Leo J. Chance had slipped into The Ecliptic World undetected. Just outside the landing port from behind a stack of cargo containers, he waited for the perfect time to strike. A blast came from Chance's pistol, cutting through the night like a tracer. It just missed the landing struts of the OS payload section and hit a storage container with a bright flash, catching everyone by surprise. Another blast scattered the crew, as they unholstered their own proton pistols and dropped to the ground. Captain Jones' face went dark with rage as he yelled out in disbelief.

"Who the hell is firing at us at a time like this?"

"I don't know, but keep an eye out," shouted Chief Mack, as they began to search the darkness outside the reach of the payload section's landing lights. "We can't stay pinned down like this. Let's make a run for it."

"We're with you," answered Anjum. "Let's go."

The first to rise from position was Lt. Martinez, followed by Sarwar, while Captain Jones and Tapia waited for the chief to give the word.

"OK, let's move." They all ran for the ramp door about fifty meters away. Lt. Martinez took the lead followed by Win, Tapia, Sarwar and Seth, with Jack taking up the rear. Still keeping a watchful eye on the group, Chance quickly moved away from the loading containers and ran behind an explosives storage facility looking for a better angle. Chance smiled as he took aim at a new target, the son of his former commander. His blood boiled with revenge.

"I have you now," said Chance pulling the trigger on his pistol. The burst found its mark, hitting Captain Jones in the abdomen, knocking him down, propelling him across the rough tarmac. With a victorious glint in his eye, Chance and his men quickly regrouped and ran in the direction of their ship.

"It's Chance. He's here," Tapia yelled out.

"Chance," the chief ordered. "Get him!"

Jessica and Anjum fired a series of proton bursts at Chance and his men and were soon joined by the others.. The bursts hit the storage facility causing a huge explosion that rocked the port.

Debris rained down like a torrent, forcing them to take cover. Jessica, Win and Anjum ran back to aid the crippled captain as he shivered in pain. He managed to look up at them and whisper through clenched teeth, "I hope you got the bastard."

With so much smoke and wreckage, there was no way to know if Chance survived the explosion. Anjum leaned over his fallen comrade.

"Hey Jack, are you OK, buddy?"

"I'll be fine, just get as many people as you can inside and get out of here."

"Yes, but you need a doctor," said Anjum.

"I'll live," said Jack.

"Sarwar, take care of him until we get back," Chief Mack ordered.

"No problem Chief, he's in good hands."

The others turned to run the rest of the way to the ramp door and help the people that were arriving. Anjum rested the captain's head on his lap and tore off part of his uniform to dress his wound. Jack cringed and writhed in pain.

A group of about thirty people ran toward the OutStar. It was one of the last ships left that was not filled to capacity. Jessica, Tapia and Seth motioned the survivors to move quickly.

"Come on, come on, move, people, move," Tapia shouted in a loud and determined voice, corralling the people into the ship.

There were hundreds of people in the main cargo hold alone. Doctor Mutara had set up a triage to care for the survivors with serious injuries or viral contamination from coming within close proximity to the creatures.

"Doctor," Tapia informed her, "Jack has been shot and it looks pretty bad. He's just below the ramp." Odette flinched, but made no move.

A continuous beeping came over Jessica's COMlink. She quickly pulled the unit off her belt.

"Martinez."

"It's Win. I'm taking off in the main ship. I have a full load of people on board and I want you to get the payload section out of here before one of those things reaches the landing port."

"I hear you Chief. We will be under way in a few. Martinez out."

Immediately, the main ship's thrusters came to life with a roar and the vibrations traveled down through the structure of the payload section to the ground. Achieving lift-off status, the main ship slowly moved vertically away from the top of the payload section and into the darkened sky, its four vertical thrusters blazing with blue and red flames. It changed its vector to move in the direction to the mountains.

Back on the tarmac, where the injured captain lay bleeding, two looming, blue-hazed shadows, black against black, almost hidden by the night, hovered overhead. They had broken through one of the colony buildings, splitting it in half with a lighting-like ray, causing an explosion like a fountain of blinding fire through the sky. They seemed unstoppable in their quest, using their deadly tentacles to grab and devour everything that moved, making their way toward the landing port. Tapia and Seth turned at the sound of the explosion.

"Oh hell," Jessica said, as she and Seth ran back toward their friend. Tapia ran inside the OutStar to supervise the rescue. Jessica took her transport case from around her chest.

"Here, you might need this in case something pops up." She placed the case beside the captain on the tarmac.

The bone-jarring pounding of the creature's approach grew nearer. The captain instructed his friends.

"You better get the hell out of here. Those things are moving faster than before."

Jessica turned her head, blinking the sweat out of her eyes and estimated the distance from the creature to the OutStar. She turned back to face him.

"Anjum, lets see if we can move Jack inside the ship before those things reach us."

As they grabbed the captain's shoulders to pull him up, Jack cried out in pain, "It's too late. We'll never make it in time. Anjum, go before we lose the ship and everybody on board."

Frantic seconds ticked by as the creatures advanced. Anjum gently lay Jack's head on the tarmac and ran grudgingly toward the ship.

"Don't worry. I'll be back with help."

"You better," Jack replied. "Hey, you're in charge now, so please, no more tests!" Jack laughed, wincing in pain.

"Where is the fun in that? Just keep safe until I return," Anjum called back as he raced to the OutStar.

Running up the ramp door, he hit the control pad as he passed the hatchway causing the hydraulics to come to life with a whine. The ramp lifted from the tarmac closing with a solid thud. The injured Jack, Seth and Jessica tried to move away from the engine-blast of the OutStar payload section. Jack took his arm and placed it around Jess's shoulder as she gently maneuvered herself to a standing position. For a woman her size, she was very strong.

"Are you OK? We have to move now just a little faster, before the engines ignite," warned Jessica. Jack nodded. The engine warming sequence began. Jessica and Jack made it just far enough away to escape the engine blast. They joined Seth as they watched the OutStar begin the departure sequence. The main vertical thruster engines made the ground rumble. The landing struts retracted slowly into their compartments as the ship reached an altitude of about one hundred meters.

With a flash, a silvery tendril shot out from the one of the hovering smoke-beasts and wrapped itself around the rear landing-strut just before it disappeared into the hatch. The ship pulled against the creature, but could not escape. Emergency signals flashed on and off inside the ship. The force of the struggle on the power systems overloaded circuits and the main power began to fluctuate violently. The ship tilted at forty-five degree angle and the crew was flung about the cabin, grabbing in vain for support.

"What the hell is happening?" asked Sarwar. "Main viewscreen," Anjum ordered. "Damn it, one of those things has wrapped itself around our rear strut."

"Sir, main power is failing." Noise filled the command center as technicians rushed around trying to restore main power.

"Can we sever the tendril by firing one of our canons?" yelled Ensign Ryan.

"No, it's too close, I have something else in mind," said Anjum.

"Commander Roberts and Lt. Martinez are firing at the tentacle, Lt. Sarwar"

"Good, let me know if they free us. Computer, go to manual control. Ensign, I will take over from here." Anjum moved quickly to the navigation console and maneuvered the controls with great accuracy, but the ship still lost ground against the strength of the cloud creature. System after system went off-line and a gas leak broke through the inner-bulkhead wall of the command center. In the cargo bay, Dr. Mutara and her skeleton staff tried to keep everybody calm, but Odette's thoughts were with Jack.

The grip of the tendril got tighter. The hydraulic system grinded and whirred and lines that ran from the control box began to short-out, snapping the cables like threads in a matter of seconds. The strut started to loosen. The OutStar reversed its thrusters, giving itself some slack against the creature's tendril.

"What kind of maneuver is this?" Ensign Ryan asked.

"Don't worry, just testing out one of my theories." A grumble rippled through the command crew.

"Excuse me gentlemen, cut the chatter and tell me if we have power to the auxiliary systems?"

"Sir, they're still in the green, but you'd better apply your theory now before we lose these power levels."

"Go to full power on the aux on my signal. Timing is of the essence, so be ready, we won't get another chance at this."

Inside the command center, the image on the screen was unstable and unclear, but Anjum stayed calm and at ease. He focused his attention on his timing for when the creature exerted more energy to try and pull the craft down. The repair crew entered the command center and extinguished what was left of the electrical fires.

Outside, Seth and Jessica fired again at the tentacle, but with no success.

"It's not working this time." Seth ran out of the docking bay to try another angle. Jack monitored what was happening from the ground.

"Remember how the concentrated blast to the core worked on UC-788? Maybe if we concentrate our beams on the tentacle, we can free them," Jack said, struggling to his feet, ignoring the pain in his side.

"Captain, let's do it," Jessica agreed with a determined voice. The three comrades aimed their pistols and fired continuously from a distance of about one hundred meters. Their proton blasts sliced through the night with blinding speed hitting the tentacle just below the strut. The creature began to loosen its hold.

"It's working! Damn it, it's working!"

It was too early for celebration. As the creature lurched back, trying to unravel itself from the landing strut, another tentacle lashed out, slashing Seth across the back and sending him to the ground on his face. The electrical tendril wrapped around the legs of the commander and lifted him into the air.

Jack and Jessica diverted their fire to the tentacle that snaked around Seth. He screamed in pain as the powerful muscle seared his skin.

The OutStar was pulled down again and at that moment Anjum gave the signal to go to full auxiliary power. With the force of its thrusters screaming with extra power, the landing strut ripped away from the ship, severing the gripping tentacle. With smoke trailing from its ruptured strut, the OutStar payload section lurched forward and achieved lift-off, bringing cheers and sighs of relief from everyone in the command center.

Anjum, filled with anger and frustration, wanted to get even. He ordered Tapia, who was manning the cannons to target the alien that tried to destroy them. Tapia fired with full power. The two cannons let out a burst of proton energy that found their mark, hitting the creature's blazing core. It then exploded like a bomb, sending thick, nightmarish, black smoke and particles of alien-matter bursting through the sky. Little to Anjum's knowledge Seth, was still attached to the beast.

"Seth!" called Jack and Jessica. They watched as his limp body sailed through the air, landing in a crumpled pile about fifty meters away. Lt. Martinez ran to his side, but she was too late.

Anjum, Tapia and the rest of the flight crew focused their attention on taking the crippled ship and its passengers to the outer mountain region to safety.

"Damn." A worried look crossed Anjum's face.

"What's wrong?" Tapia asked.

"We can't land the ship because…"

"Yes," Tapia cut in abruptly, "I already know the problem. Our solution is proper weight distribution. I'll contact Doctor Mutara and tell her to move as many of the people as we can from the cargo area to the front of the ship so we don't bottom out in the rear."

Unfortunately for Jack and Jessica, they had attracted the attention of the other creature in the chaos. It moved in their direction, its tendrils flaring, giving them had no time to mourn the loss of their friend.

They aimed their pistols at the oncoming alien and cut loose with a series of blasts. Suddenly, Jack and Jessica heard voices and the sound of feet coming from behind them, the sound almost lost in the deafening barrage of noise and smoke. They turned and to their surprise and relief, saw Win and two security officers quickly approaching with their proton weapons drawn, ready to join in the firefight.

"Win, we've lost Seth." Jessica reached out and took his hand.

"What?! No! I came back to get you…it can't be."

A jolt of reality surged through them. Their conversation was cut short by a loud rumble that pierced the putrid, smoke-filled air. They backed up and unleashed all the firepower at their command at the relentless alien horror moving in their direction. Lurking in the shadows, Leo J. Chance watched their struggle with glee.

A force that could only occur in a nightmare continued to charge its way across the planet and put

Capitol One, like so many others before it, in its death grip; a force that would be reckoned with, one way or another, before all beings in the known star-systems were taken over by evil.

RICHARD ANTHONY CRISCUOLA HAS BEEN working for a major airline for over 13 years. He enjoys traveling, photography, model-making and skiing. He lives and works in New York City.

Sam McPherson has been working in the music industry for the last 20 years. He is a gifted model-maker, set designer and prop master. He lives and works in New York City.

Richard and Sam met eighteen years ago. They have been writing and collaborating for nearly 10 years. This is their first book and they are currently working on the sequel to *Dark Discovery*.

For your next **Big Production**
Look no further!

Join Today!

- Support Staff
- Talent Representation
- Advertsing/Publicity
- Consulting/Event Mgmt
- Celebrity Procurement
- Legal Svcs/Contracts
- Graphic Design
- Website Design/Hosting

Celebrity ENTERTAINMENT

www.CelebrityEntertainment.org